Resolutions

Resolutions

an anthology

Edited by Debz Hobbs-Wyatt and Gill James

Bridge House

British Library Cataloguing in Publication Data

A Record of this Publication is available from the British
Library

ISBN 978-1-914199-10-3

This edition published 2021 by Bridge House Publishing
Manchester, England

Contents

Introduction

It is never easy choosing stories for a collection; stories that standout in their own right and that will also work together. You might think after thirteen years of publishing anthologies it would get easier. It never does and sometimes it seems the standard just keeps getting better. Over the years we have developed a signature style of story that is 'Bridge House' though not always easy to define. You just know it when you read it. It's something that has developed over time and been shaped largely by the lovely writers who continue to contribute interesting and thought-provoking stories. This is the second year running we have accepted stories anonymously for this collection, and so it's lovely when we still see some of the same authors being accepted – alongside new ones of course. We also used a submissions manager. This has made the whole process smoother but has also introduced some fresh challenges. However, we must change with the times.

Every year we choose a *loose* theme often linked to the festive season which is when our collections are published. Some writers use the theme literally and for this year we had a lot of submission about New Year resolutions, some of which did make it into the final selection. But often we find that writers find varied and interesting, highly original ways to interpret the theme. When we chose 'resolutions' it could in effect be any story since all stories need a resolution. But we were delighted with how the authors have given more thought to it than that.

There was a variety of submissions and we were hard-pressed to select the best! We looked for: story, good writing, interpretation of theme and professionalism. All of the stories submitted had those elements. How we came to this final selection was not easy but I am sure you will all agree the stories work wonderfully together.

The only downside is that often we have to reject some great stories, but perhaps they don't quite hit the mark, or there is one that just pips it to the post. Sometimes when we have similar stories, we opt for the one that works best, and also of course we have to stand back and look at how it comes together as a collection – so we need variation to cater to readers' eclectic tastes.

We hope you enjoy how the Bridge House authors (old and new) this year have interpreted theme and thank you all for your continued support of the small press; especially in these more trying times. When we announced this theme last year, we were plunged into lockdown in the UK. It is said that in trying times community spirit lifts us up, and we can safely say, our writing community is no exception. It certainly has not hampered creative minds!

So, sit back and surrender to the Bridge House magic.

Advent Calendar

Dianne Stadhams

Day 1:

We went to church that day, me, my wife Rhonda and the dog Rhyll. I know, I know... who has a dog with a name like that... and who takes a dog to church? Rhonda does and what Rhonda wants she gets. I could have put up a fight but what's the point? A miffed wife equals a misery life. Rhyll always sides with her mistress and has been known to nip my heels to show support.

"Never... Rhyll doesn't bite. Do you my precious pooch?" my wife replied as she cuddled her mutt. "You must have got your feet under her at the wrong moment. She likes her space. You know that."

That dog gets more affection than I've ever collected... even in the early days of our getting together when sex was on the agenda.

The priest likes Rhyll and Rhonda. Rhonda does the flowers for the church. She bakes him a cake every week. So do four of the other middle-aged women in the congregation. It's a sort of best of the bake off. He's a fat, canny bastard. Always praises them equally but never in the same breath. Keeps them at their ovens, sugaring his path to heaven. Except for Lent when he loses a kilo or two. But then it's double do after as the four compete to swamp the good father with chocolate porn.

Not Carol though. She doesn't do anything for the church except turn up for services and light a candle as she leaves.

Rhonda and I never sit near Carol. She hates dogs. I asked her once if the candle was in remembrance of her husband. The look she flashed suggested her dead hubby rated right down there with dogs.

9

After church we walked home through the forest. Rhonda kept Rhyll on the lead.

"They've spotted wild boar," she explained. "We don't want Rhyll hurt. You know what those feral pigs are like."

Now that's worth a prayer. Three Hail Marys for the swine.

Back home Rhonda got out three advent calendars and placed them on the marble mantelpiece amidst the fake holly and plastic pinecones. She opened the first door on each calendar and handed me a chocolate wrapped in red foil, another for herself and to Rhyll a plain, bone-shaped chocolate.

"I thought chocolate was like poison for dogs," I said.

Rhonda smiled and replied, "Not these. I got these at the pet shop. Just for doggies. You wouldn't want my baby to miss out, would you?"

Want to make a bet?

Rhyll growled.

That damn dog is psychic.

Day 2:

I saw Carol today. She was in the delicatessen section of the supermarket. I was buying six cans of pedigree dog food.

She smiled.

I walked up to her. She smelt of lavender. She was buying French air-dried salami. It's made from pork.

Rhonda hates the French. She says it's because of what happened to her on a school trip... my lips are sealed.

Light bulb moment. Supermarket to super plan.

Day 3:

Rhyll is a cockapoo. The clue to her temperament lies in the third syllable.

Facts about poo breed dogs. They all have genes from poodles. Poodles were originally hunting dogs. They're intelligent... so Rhyll's breeder said.

10

If Rhyll is typical she's inherited the possessive, arrogant, finicky traits of the poodle combined with the yappiness and stench of cocker spaniels.

Rhonda wants Rhyll to be a mother.

Bitches... both of them.

Day 4:

"Are you stalking me?" Carol laughed.

"It's a free forest." I smiled. "Walk this way often?"

"Most days. I'm fascinated by the wild boar."

"Me too," I lied.

Note to self. Research feral pigs.

Day 5:

Did you know pigs are omnivores? That means they eat anything... even poo.

Day 6:

I got our credit card statement today. Our money is held in a joint account. I earn it. Rhonda spends it. Last month she spent £400 on hairdressing. £100 pounds kept her roots blonde. The other £300 meant Rhyll smelt like any pampered pooch would if it had a conditioned wash and blow dry every Saturday... in preparation for Mass.

I fed Rhyll a real chocolate drop... after the advent calendar doggy-do one... when Rhonda wasn't looking. I swear Rhyll winked.

There are many ways to skin a cat... or a cockapoo.

Watch this space mutt head.

Day 7:

I bought a lavender bush today. Rhonda was furious.

"I hate lavender," she shouted.

I know.

11

"Lavender represents purity, silence, devotion serenity, grace and calmness," I replied.

"Where did you learn that?" Rhonda asked.

Carol told me when I said her perfume blew me away.
I shrugged.

My sources are secret.

Rhyll sat on my slippers and farted.

Day 8:

"Why are you interested in wild boar?" I asked Carol when I accidently on purpose collided with her in the forest.

"Long story," she said.

"Extended walk," I replied. "Tell me all."

"I thought you said you were into wild pigs," Carol said while collecting dropped pine cones and loading them into her lime green rucksack. She loves colour, my Carol does. Today she is wearing a hot pink puffa jacket and turquoise laces in her walking boots. Her red hair is curly, piled high like a pineapple. I can imagine her as an exotic fairy blown off course from the tropics.

"You tell me yours and I'll show you mine," I replied.

I'm not sure she heard because she launched straight into a lecture. Everything from legislation on wild mammals to European distribution statistics regarding herds from Germany to the Forest of Dean... a right bore on boars.

"Nothing I can add," I said.

Day 9:

Cockapoos suffer from eye and joint problems. Rhyll has had a number of visits to the vet over the last six weeks. Today I got the bill... £500. Seems that mutt has got glaucoma in her its eyes, hip dysplasia and suspect kidneys.

Rhonda is beside herself with angst.

So am I. That bitch is going to cost me £150 per month in medication for the rest of her life. That's in addition to the grooming.

Rhonda tells me she's heard of a therapist who specialises in dog massage.

What can I research on dog euthanasia?

I feed Rhyll a large bar of high percentage, cocoa chocolate when I take her for a walk.

Rhonda gives her a cuddle and the dog choc from the canine Advent calendar.

Note that star in the East mutt head? This wise man has your number.

Day 10:

Rhonda went to clean the church after we had the daily offerings from the advent calendar with our morning coffee.

I drove to four supermarkets and bought a six pack of large sweet corn cans from each.

"Why did you buy so many?" Rhonda asked.

"Organic fertilizer," I replied.

"So how does that work out alongside the slug pellets and weed killer?" Rhonda snapped.

Day 11:

I went to mid-week Eucharist with Rhonda… and Rhyll.

When the priest talked about the communion ritual with the bread and wine representing the body and blood of Christ I felt quite uplifted. My very own sign that I was on the right path.

Halleluiah!

Rhonda smiled as I drank the wine and held my hand afterwards in the pew.

Rhyll snarled silently, her mutt lips taught with resentment at Rhonda's touch.

Amen!

Day 12:

Did you know that sweet corn is popular in hog baits, because hogs can easily recognize the smell? Corn ferments after it's soaked for several days, creating a smell that will attract hogs but keep other animals, such as deer, away.

Day 13:

"I really like walking and talking with you, Carol," I said, "I mean REALLY, REALLY like."

"I enjoy it too," said Carol.

"Perhaps we could have a drink together at the Miners' Arms after our walk?" I suggested.

Carol replied, "I know you follow me."

Was that look on her face a flirt or a smirk?

"I like you," I said.

"I like you too."

"Then it's a date?"

Day 14:

Another day, another bar of chocolate for Rhyll when Rhonda wasn't looking.

Rhyll cocked her head to one side but quaffed it anyway.

Score one to me.

Day 15:

The highlight of my day was watching Carol photographing wild boar. I hid behind the oak trees.

Watch and learn.

Day 16:

Rhonda baked a cake for the priest and took fresh holly and mistletoe to the church.

Was the priest going to get lucky and score a kiss?

I went to check the sweet corn... fermenting nicely.

Day 17:

Rhyll is getting used to our clandestine arrangement. I gave her two blocks of finest Columbian dark chocolate today.

Day 18:

I suggested a long walk in the woods with Rhyll to Rhonda. She wasn't sure it was a good idea given Rhyll was off her food.

"Fresh air and a good run will do her a power of good," I argued.

"We'd better keep her on the lead. I hear the wild boar are on the rampage," Rhonda advised.

Live in hope.

"You're in an odd mood today," Rhonda mused when I told her of a new route through the forest that I had discovered.

Last supper... for you and the pigs.

Day 19:

I went to the Miners' Arms. I spotted the hot pink puffa jacket straight away and headed to the table.

"Liz will be pleased to put a face to your name," Carol replied as she carried a pint back from the bar.

"Who's Liz?"

"My girlfriend, she owns the pub. I met her through the Association of Shooting and Conservation."

Confused? Perfection is hard to imagine.

Day 20:

I reported her missing to the police.

"Your wife done this before?" they asked.

"She has had her moments," I agreed, "but she usually lets me know when she'll be back."

"She got family she might go to?" asked the police.

"No, there's just us... and our dog."

They asked about our social life.

"Jealous type?"

"No, not really. There are more women than men in our congregation. Rhonda and I talk to everyone."

I left it with them. They contacted me later in the day and said the priest had mentioned I was friendly with church goer Carol.

Confession good for soul, you pious prick?

"Carol doesn't have much to do with Rhonda outside of services," I said.

"But you do?" asked the police.

"We often bump into each other when we're out walking."

"You see this Carol without your wife around?" they asked.

"I've had a drink with her in the pub," I admitted.

"Your missus upset about that?"

"Not really," I replied. "Carol's gay."

Day 21:

I read on the Internet that if you cut up a corpse into six pieces, sixteen hungry pigs can go through 90 kilos of meat in about eight minutes.

Rhonda weighed 60 kilos. The sweet corn slop weighed a kilo. I just spread it over her body, like a balm. The boar tusks were more efficient than a meat cleaver.

Damn dog escaped. Took me half an hour to catch her.

16

I took Rhyll back to the house and fed her chocolate...
a lot of it.
Comfort food.

Day 22:

Rhyll rolled in wild boar poo during our walk.
Whoever said a dog is a man's best friend lied.
I doused Rhyll in lavender oil when we returned to the
house.
Sweet revenge.
Rhyll bit me.
Bitch!
I gave her my your-days-are-numbered look.
Rhyll rolled on the newly planted lavender bush and
squashed it.
No dinner for Rhyll but I gave her the dog chocolate
from the advent calendar along with a chocolate laxative
for humans.
Who laughs last laughs longest.

Day 23:

No news of Rhonda, the police informed me.
Three members from the congregation visited.
Carol didn't.

Day 24:

I went to Midnight Mass. The priest mentioned me in his
prayers.
Another ritual... whatever makes him happy.
People mostly avoided my eyes when they offered their
condolences.
"I'm sure she'll be back. Menopause is a difficult time
for women," one of the cake bakers said.
"May the Lord be with you," the priest blessed.

I sincerely hope He leaves me alone.

"How is poor Rhyll coping?" another of the cake bakers asked.

Home alone yapping her head hoarse.

"Rhyll will always be welcome in my church," the priest whispered.

Dog collars united.

"You should have brought her to mass," someone said. "She's such a sensitive soul."

Since when did poo dogs get souls?

Day 25:

Rhyll and I started with the last chocolate from all three advent calendars. Doors opened sesame. No more surprises. Rhyll got double dos and ate Rhonda's. No need to be wasteful.

I switched on the television to watch the carol service. The dog hates singing. I turned the volume up full blast.

Silent Night.

It seemed a shame to waste a good festive dinner. So I shared some with Rhyll. Fed it to her on Rhonda's plate, turkey with all the trimmings. I want to fatten Rhyll up. Those wild boar deserve a decent morsel for a good New Year's Day.

She barked when the doorbell rang.

Oh God, please don't let it be that damned priest.

The two policemen at the door didn't like Rhyll either. She snapped at their heels.

Fat lot of luck, mutt head. These pigs wear serious boot leather. Lose a tooth!

The two policemen asked to come in. Seems they want to ask me some more questions about my absent wife.

Hors d'oeuvres officers... wild boar salami? Special Christmas resolution... recipe courtesy of Rhonda.

18

About the author

Dianne Stadhams is an Australian, resident in the UK, who works globally in marketing and project management. With a PhD in visual anthropology she has used creative tools – drama, dance, radio, video – to empower others in some of the world's poorest nations. She believes passionately that the arts are valuable tools to promote social cohesion, provoke debate and influence attitudes, mind sets and actions. www.stadhams.com

Alex DuBon's Resolution

Jon Hepworth

Alex DuBon stood by the window. He hung onto each moment, surprised at the importance of each second when death is near.

He gazed at the thin strips of lead that crisscrossed the window dividing it into small diamond shapes. He noticed small patches of dust that had gathered on the lower corner of each small pane of glass. Must be murder to clean. He ran the fingers of his right hand along the bottom of the oak frame that surrounded the window. He felt the corrugated roughness of the wood grain; it reminded him of the ridges left in the sand by the departing tide.

They would probably send his brother Sam for him. Why did it have to be Sam of all people? He disliked Sam, too smooth, too correct.

He leant over and turned the fleur-de-lee catch. The hinges groaned and threw out tiny curls of rust as he pushed the window open a few inches. He felt the warm air on his face as it crept into the room. The quiet was disrupted by the sound of birds' calls that had echoed across the garden and now entered the room. A syringa bush grew beside the window and its white flowers gave off a heavy scent that invaded his breathing.

Some roses grew in the flowerbed below the window. Alex watched as a butterfly settled on a bloom and spread its wings wide as it basked in the sunlight, the deep colours of red, black and white glowing with life. It flew away, becoming ever smaller until it was swallowed up in the summer sky. Alex envied such freedom, such simplicity.

He tried to drink in every sensation that each second could provide, as if, somehow he could stop time.

He dropped his hand to his side and stood still as he looked across the lawn to the vegetable garden. What a wretched patch of ground.

Alex had been told that his grandfather had done a lot of cash deals during the war and had buried wads of money in jam jars in the vegetable garden. His grandfather had then died before he was able to tell anyone exactly where and how deep he had buried the money. As a result Alex, as a young boy, had spent hours digging all over the ground and when he had dug it over once, he dug it all over again but this time much deeper. Often at dusk his young silhouette could be seen bent over a spade. Alex's father had roared with laughter as he told Alex the truth. The truth was that there was no buried money, but that the story had been a very effective way of ensuring the ground was well dug. From that moment Alex hated his father and each time the story was retold the hatred grew.

Now his father was dying. Dying in the bedroom directly above where he was standing. They were no more than ten feet apart, divided only by floor joists, a ceiling and years of resentment.

He heard the door open behind him and the quiet steps of rubber-soled shoes. The smell of eau de cologne told him that it was Sam.

"You've got to see the old man."

"Why?"

"He's dying – he wants to see you – to make it up."

"Did he say that?"

"Not exactly!"

"Well – there you are then!"

"Please, Alex – he really does want to see you. Seeing you will help. He's very distressed."

"It's too late for all that."

They were interrupted by the sound of steps and then Aunt Doe was standing in the doorway.

He's..." she paused, her voice unsteady. Her chin quivered with emotion. "He's gone," she whispered.

Alex lent over and closed the window to shut out the sounds of life. The house was silent.

The room suddenly seemed to be a sepulchre, invaded by death. The three figures stood like lifeless statues, sharing in their sense of shock, in their struggle for comprehension.

Sam looked on with disdain and contempt.

"Will you see him now – now that he is dead?" said Sam.

The will was found a few days later. Everyone was very disappointed. Their father's supposed fortune had disappeared; he had obviously been living off his capital for a long time. At least it would reduce the inheritance tax problems. The house went to Sam and the contents of the house to Aunt Doe. Alex was left the vegetable garden. Sam offered to buy the vegetable garden but Alex decided to keep it.

The years went by and Alex forgot about the plot of land that he owned until Sam decided to get married and asked Alex to the wedding.

The reception was in the house and Alex found himself standing by that window again. He leaned forward and opened it. Well-oiled hinges swung open in silence. He looked over at the vegetable garden.

"Quite a mess – isn't it," said Sam who had come over to him.

"Have a look at this aerial picture – it will show you what it used to look like – I had it taken when I inherited the house."

Next to the window was a gilt framed picture of the house and gardens. "Very nice!" said Alex in a flat voice.

Sam moved on. Alex looked at the photo – strange what aerial photos will pick up. Patterns not easily seen from the ground. There was a dark pattern in the middle of the vegetable garden. Alex could see the darkened outline of a cross.

"The cross marks the place where the treasure is buried!" thought Alex and he smiled as he remembered the time he had read Treasure Island.

Somewhere in the recesses of his mind a hidden thought took shape. Alex was unaware of it until it burst into his conscious mind with the power of a tidal wave. He gasped for breath. His face crumpled into a thousand harrowing lines. He stretched out a hand to the window to steady himself.

It couldn't be, could it! Life just wasn't like that.

Sam was relieved to hear that Alex had decided to tidy up the vegetable garden. Alex disappeared for days behind a wall of brambles, stinging nettles, fat hen, docks and some saplings that had taken root.

At exactly one metre he hit the first glass jar. There was a smashing sound as the spade sliced through the glass. Then another and another. There were twenty-five jars full of sovereigns – gold sovereigns.

The last jar had a note in. All the note said was '*Hi Alex – sorry for the pain – couldn't bear to let the tax man get all this. Thought you would work it out – your loving father*'.

About the author
Jon has been writing fiction and non-fiction stories for some twenty years, since he has retired. He has had various articles published in the farming press when working as a farming consultant, and has had four short stories published by CaféLit. He lives in East Sussex.

Benny

Topher George

Benny had the kind of smile that your mom had after the divorce papers were handed to her that August. It's strained at the sides, like two thin pieces of wire pulling the corners up slightly. If you didn't know Benny, you would probably have looked straight past it, but I didn't, because I did know Benny.

I knew him when he rode his Redline into the side of Mr. Harpers Cadillac and legged it all the way home. Hell, I knew him when he pulled his trousers to his ankles and flashed Principle Myers on his way to first period. Benny was the very definition of the life of my teenage years. The two of us were joined at the hip. Benny was rebellious, and I was the guy with an escape plan.

One summer. That's all it took. Just one summer.

When he came back to town after it happened, I remember wondering how much it had taken of him. I wanted percentages. I wanted to know what percentage of Benny had made it back. I remember sitting on the back porch a few hours after he arrived home. He was tired, as though his bones weighed more now than they did then; as though they were weighted with grief. The once quiet house was now filled with busy adults who seemingly knew more about the task of stocking his fridge with home cooked meals than sitting with Benny amidst the grim reality of what had happened. We had all met grief before, but when he is a guest at someone else's home, we seem to forget his name.

We didn't speak for a while. I sat beside him as he lit up a cigarette, smoked it, rubbed it out, and lit another. We had spent countless evenings out on this porch, secretly

24

smoking cigarettes, eating pizza and talking rubbish. I don't think there was anything Benny didn't know about me, and until now, I thought I knew everything there was to know about Benny.

"My grandparents are moving down here on Thursday. They say they want to keep my life as normal as it can be" Benny finally said, a bitter laugh stifled at the end of his words. We were silent again. Both thinking about what a normal life for Benny would look like now. If it could be normal at all.

"I hate him" Benny whispered, his words were so sharp that they sliced the air around us into fragments. It was there, just behind his mechanical smile, the unadulterated hatred of his father.

"Benny, what happened?" I asked tentatively. I had read a version of that night in the paper, and had a watered-down version given to me by my parents, but no one but Benny really knew what had happened.

He didn't say anything for a long time. I felt a sense of dread that I had become just another curious person insistent on asking him all the questions he was trying hard to avoid. I held my knees and looked straight ahead. If he told me, would I be able to sit with that? Would the details be too gruesome? Would it haunt me the way it was clearly haunting him?

"He killed my mother, and then he killed himself," Benny replied, his tone stark and void of any discernible emotion. The admission fell onto me like a ton of bricks, the papers were telling the truth. It wasn't that I didn't believe the words that were printed, it was just… I had met Frank Holland.

He had taught me little league, he had taken Benny and I into the city to our first gig; I had spent as much time with Frank Holland as I did my own father.

25

"Why?" it was the only word playing on repeat in my head, I hadn't even noticed it slip through my lips. I was sure it was the same question that had been going around in circles in Benny's head too and I wasn't sure either of us would find an answer that would have this make any more sense.

"He had been unwell for a while now. At first he was sad all the time, and then he got angry; it was like he was another person completely by the end. I just kept thinking he would get through it eventually, I didn't think..." he stopped short, holding his breath to steady himself before emotion swept through him like a cascade.

"He loved you, Benny. And your Mum loved you. I don't know why things happened the way they did but I do know they both loved you" I said nudging his shoulder with mine, giving each other a teary eyed smile.

I had no idea why Frank would do what he did, or how he could have done what he did. I hope I never understood. The only thing I knew was that Benny was here now and he wouldn't ever be alone. He was as much a part of my family as I was his, and right now he needed to feel a sense of home.

"You said your grandparents weren't arriving for a few days. Why don't you grab a few things and stay with us?" he looked up at me and for the first time I saw the small child in him; the fear and the desperation to be held. His lip quivered and he nodded.

As if she had heard our conversation, my mother walked over from across the garden where she had been talking with Benny's neighbour. I admired my mother, she gave Benny a soft rub on his shoulder but she didn't pry.

"Hey, Mom, can Benny stay over until his grandparents get here?" I asked, as if her answer wasn't obvious to anyone within stone's throw.

26

"Of course, dear. Listen, I know everyone has made you a bunch of meals, but I hate to think what Mrs. Gray put in that pie." she said with a laugh, scrunching up her face up in mock disgust.

"How about we order a pizza and you boys can stay in the den?" Benny smiled and looked a shade lighter than when I first saw him. For the first time, his smile was a little more genuine. We may never know why it happened, but we were resolute in rebuilding our family around Benny.

About the author

Topher George is an emerging author from Victoria, Australia.

For him, there are no themes, subjects or stories that cannot be told. Between the gritty and the gruesome are the bones of life, and there is where you will find Topher. Often ankle deep in subjects that are deemed uncomfortable, Topher pulls you in, blurs the lines of morality and humanises the inhumane in all of us.

Conflict Resolution Management

Tony Domaille

"So, what are you going to do about it?"

If a little spittle hadn't accompanied her question, I might have remained zoned out. I'm good at that. I can look people right in the eye and appear to be transfixed by their words. What I'm actually doing is zoning them out and daydreaming. But a little spittle did hit my cheek. That's how I caught the question, though hopefully nothing else.

"Well?" she said, whilst I was trying to formulate an answer without her knowing I hadn't been listening.

"I'm going to move Heaven and Earth to get a resolution for you, Eileen," I said.

She rolled her eyes. "It's Ellen."

"Yes, of course." I rolled my own eyes in self-deprecation. "Leave it with me, Ellen," I ushered her out the door.

Thankfully, my secretary is brilliant. She does listen. All I needed to do was give her a call and ask her what on Earth Eileen, or whatever her name was, had come to see me about. How important could it be? I'm a floor manager in a warehouse where two dozen women, and our newly employed gender fluid Latvian, sew shirts together. The biggest crisis I had managed in my nine years there was a coffee machine break-down.

"Remind me, Jean," I said. "What did Erin come to see me about?"

Jean laughed. "Mike, she just left your office… and it's Ellen."

"Well, you know how it is."

"I know how you are. I'd better come and speak to you."

When Jean came into my office, I expected her to gently

scold me for not listening. As it was, she came in looking quite sombre.

"Oh, God, was she complaining about the rough toilet paper in the ladies again?" I asked.

Jean shook her head. "I can't believe she could be in here for ten minutes and you didn't listen to a word."

I shrugged. "She doesn't know I wasn't listening. I told her I'd sort it."

"It?"

"Yes. Whatever *it* is. What's her problem?"

Jean sat heavily in the chair opposite me and sighed. "It's a serious matter, Mike. She's complaining she's been sexual harassed by Jim. How are you going to sort that out?"

"Jim? Our Jim?"

"Yes, our Jim," said Jean. "Your boss, my boss, everybody's boss, here."

This wasn't good. I am sure that being sexually harassed by a man twice your age, and weight, is unpleasant. I am a modern man and know that inappropriate behaviour in the workplace is… well, it's inappropriate. It's the kind of thing that needs to be stamped out. People should do all they can to make perpetrators feel outcasts. I'm all for draconian action, but I really didn't fancy taking it with the man who employed me. What had I said to whatshername? *"I'm going to move Heaven and Earth to get a resolution for you."* I wished I had been listening and then I could have said something much less likely to raise any expectations.

"So, what are you going do about it?" asked Jean.

I considered going long-term sick. Stress would do it, and I certainly felt stressed. But then I couldn't just walk away from my responsibilities. And then I shuddered at what it would be like looking for a new job at fifty-six, after Jim sacked me for daring to question his behaviour. This was so much worse than the coffee machine crisis of 2015.

"He is a letch," said Jean. "I catch him staring at my…" she trailed off.

I took a deep breath. "I'm going to have to deal with it."

"Good luck with that, then," said Jean and off she went to make some coffee.

I spent the next few minutes trying to recall my Conflict Resolution Management course. That didn't go well, so I tried rehearsing in my head what I might say to Jim. I came up with several approaches, but all of them were bound to meet a "*You're fired,*" response. I couldn't see how I could deal with the matter without becoming a casualty.

Have you ever been lost for what to do and then suddenly had an idea that would mark you as a genius? No? Me neither – not until that moment when Karlis walked past my office window. In a nano-second I knew what to do. I rushed to my door and stopped our newest employee in the corridor.

"Yes, Mr Mike," he said, in his pronounced Latvian accent.

"Just step into my office."

"What I do wrong?" he asked.

"Nothing, Karlis, nothing. But there is something you can help me with."

"You want your shirt sewn?"

"No, Karlis… thank you. No, I wanted to ask you a question. Well, several actually. Do you mind?"

Karlis frowned. "No, I no think I mind."

"Great," I said. "I was just wondering when you were planning to be a girl again. I see you are a boy… a bloke today, and I do quite understand that you don't sort of roster which days you will be… identifying, that's the word, isn't it… identifying as male or female, but as you have been a bloke all this week, I wondered if you might be a girl again soon?"

Karlis looked stunned. "Why you ask?"

And then I told him why I was asking.

My plan worked perfectly. When Karlis next identified as a girl, they came into work looking frankly gorgeous. Then I sent my Latvian secret weapon, fully briefed and carrying a hidden recording device, on an errand to Jim's office. The inevitable happened. Jim was inappropriate.

Karlis then declared to Jim that they were gender fluid, though born male. After that it was very straightforward for Karlis to convince Jim they would tell the world he had made a pass if he didn't immediately mend his ways. Producing the recording was the killer move.

Funnily enough, Jim went long-term sick with stress. It wouldn't surprise me if he takes early retirement.

Ellen was happy because Jim was gone. Karlis seemed happy enough. After all, they had been convincing as a female and helped their friends and colleagues. I guess the bonus I gave them must have helped too.

Jean was hugely impressed that I had found a way to resolve a very tricky situation, though she did have words of caution. "I bet you'll listen more carefully next time one of the girls comes to speak to you," she said.

I nodded. "Yes, it did teach me a lesson. I almost committed myself to something I couldn't deliver."

"Thank goodness for Karlis," she laughed. "Problems don't come any bigger."

Actually, Jean was wrong because then my phone rang. She looked at me quizzically as I listened to what I was told, and when I put the phone down, she couldn't wait to ask. "What was that about? I can tell by your face that something is wrong."

"That was the HR director at head office," I said. "I'm being put into the Conflict Resolution Management process. She wants to come and interview me about insensitivity towards a member of the LGBT community."

About the author

Tony primarily writes for the stage and has more than twenty award winning play scripts published in the UK. He has also written short stories for CaféLit, *Your Cat Magazine* and a number of anthologies.

Fixing Champ

Helen Kreeger

He looked at the burnt meat and then at his wife. Only his tiredness and her tears held him back from yelling at her for wasting their week's ration. "All right love, don't go on so, the veg will have to do."

"Oh Albert, I don't know what's wrong with me; I lay on the settee for a quick nap, and well, I woke up and it was ruined."

"I've told you about this. If you really must sleep in the day, Mabel, turn off the blooming stove. You could of killed yourself, love." He added the last sentence in the hope of calming his wife and getting a peaceful evening. He bent down to scratch the ears of his dog. "Give it to Champ, he's always hungry."

"I'll mix it with the peelings and make it last him a few days. Poor thing. Here Champ, come and see what Mummy's got for you!"

"He's looking a bit scrawny nowadays. Did you talk to the butcher about scraps?"

"Yes, I did. You know what the old sod told me? All the scraps is what goes in the sausages. When I asked him what about the gristle and stuff, he just smiled."

"Right, no more sausages for us, Mabel! I'll ask at the place near the factory, might have better luck."

"Albert, he gave me this."

"Who?"

"That George, in the butcher's."

"Give it here then."

Albert flicked through the *Air Raid Precautions Handbook*. He'd seen one before, at the start of the war. The corner of one page was turned down, obviously meant for his attention.

"They can't make us can they, Albert?"

He closed the handbook and put it behind the clock on the mantelpiece. "No. Not yet, anyway."

"War'll be over soon, everyone says so. Come on, Albert, let's eat then we can take Champ for a walk."

"Coming, love. We'd better wait till it's properly dark though; couldn't bear to hear that old bag down the road get on her soapbox again about how our dog is eating her grandchildren's food. It's not like they'd get any more meat than is on their blooming ration cards anyway!"

After the unsatisfying meal of boiled potatoes and mashed turnips Albert prepared his pipe while Mabel did the washing up. He could hear her keeping up a steady stream of chatter with Champ and couldn't help smiling – she would have been a first-rate mother. He didn't mind so much not having children; he had his work and his mates down the pub. But it was a constant sadness for Mabel. It almost ruined their marriage. Bringing Champ into their home had helped her, given her an outlet for all that fallow mothering.

He quietly took the handbook from behind the clock and put it in his trouser pocket. "Off to the privy! We'll go for that walk when I'm finished."

"Don't be too long, Albert, Champ's waiting to go."

In the toilet Albert opened the handbook to the page that George had meant for him to read.

The 'Cash' captive bolt pistol.

Provides the speediest, most efficient and reliable means of destroying any animal, including horses, cats, and all sizes of dogs.

Recommended by HM Home Office, and approved by the RSPCA.

There was a picture of a pistol and diagrams of where to shoot an animal in the head to ensure the cleanest kill.

Albert wondered if his old army pistol would still work if he gave it a clean-up.

George and Albert used to be good friends until the talk of war became serious. People were encouraged to have their pets put down because of the fear of food shortages. Vets couldn't cope with the numbers of animals brought to them for destroying.

That bit of hysteria settled down during the first months of the war, but by then Albert and Mabel found themselves to be about the only dog owners in their area. George had had his two pedigree boxers put down even before war was declared. He said that it wasn't only humane, but patriotic to boot. He even started reporting anyone that he suspected of giving food that was fit for human consumption to their pets, knowing full well it carried a two year prison sentence.

Albert daydreamed about using the *Cash captive bolt pistol* on good old George. Instead of murder Albert took the lesser revenge, with enormous pleasure, of using the pages of the handbook instead of the sheets of newspaper hanging on a nail stuck in the back of the privy door.

The following day Albert managed to get twenty minutes off work to go to a butcher near his factory.

"You know that it's not legal to buy what's not on your card fella! We don't have nothing to do with the black market here."

"Of course, I'm not looking for anything for me. It's my dog; he's a biggun and needs a lot of food."

"They ain't supposed to eat our food! You can be done for it."

"I'm just looking for anything that you can't use. My old lady can boil it down to get a little bit of goodness out of it. He's got a brilliant pair of jaws on him; he'll manage the toughest bit of hide. I could pay a little bit."

35

"Hang on." The butcher disappeared for a couple of minutes and returned with something wrapped in newspaper.

"Here you are, fella, that'll be two bob."

"That's more than I'm allowed to buy on my card for a whole week. What's in it?"

"What does it matter? Your blooming dog won't care, or have you brought him up on steak?"

Albert noticed a nasty smell. "Don't take offence, but I want to see what my two bob gets me." He found half a jawbone, teeth embedded, two pigs' ears and bits of unidentifiable meat, all mouldy.

"This stuff'll kill my dog," Albert could barely get out without wanting to vomit.

"Don't get high and mighty with me, fella! You shouldn't even have a dog. Country ain't got enough to feed itself let alone pets."

Albert threw the package into the butcher's face while shouting, "It's not illegal to own a dog!"

The butcher picked up a cleaver. "Maybe not, but it ain't right neither. Get out of my shop or I'll get the law on you!"

Back at work Albert considered his options for Champ. The poor dog was getting thinner by the day, with little energy to run much anymore. His once thick, shiny fur was falling out in clumps. Mabel had tried to reassure him that it was Champ getting his summer coat. She didn't believe it any more than he did.

It had been a shock to both of them that so many people had given up their pets at the start of the war, especially their dogs. Mabel had said that they were just frightened, after all no one really knew how bad food shortages might get. He hadn't been so kind in his judgement of them.

Now, he had to think about what was best for Champ. Neither he nor Mabel would have any hesitation in having their much-loved dog put down by the vet if he got a terrible illness. Albert battled with the question of Champ's situation. He was always hungry, and the air raids took their toll on him. Every siren saw them carrying a terrified Champ into their Anderson shelter where he usually lost control of his bladder. It broke their hearts to see him like that. If this war lasted as long as the last one, their dog probably wouldn't make it.

It was time to put Champ's feelings above their own. Albert headed for home at the end of his shift rehearsing how he was going to persuade Mabel to part with the thing she most treasured.

"How did it go with that butcher?"

"I'll tell you later, love. What's for dinner?"

"Ooh, you'll never guess! I met that Mrs Ross from Mayeswood Road at the bakers. You know, the one with a son down in Hornchurch. She was telling me that her brother does a bit of fishing at Ferry Marsh, got a licence and everything. Well, I says to her..."

"Bloody hell, Mabel, get to the point!"

"All right, Albert, keep your hair on. Sit yourself down. Your tea'll be ready in a mo." She headed to the kitchen with a big smile on her face. He indulged Champ with a bit of chocolate he had left over from a small bar he kept in his jacket pocket. As the dog was licking the invisible leftovers on his owner's fingers, Albert couldn't help gently probing Champ's head with his free hand, finding the areas marked out in the handbook diagrams. He decided to keep his thoughts to himself till after their meal. Mabel should enjoy her happiness for a bit longer.

"What burnt offerings you got tonight, Mabel?"

"Well, come in and see for yourself."

Albert put on his best face and sat down at the kitchen table.

"Now, you cheeky blighter, how about this?"

Albert stared at the biggest piece of fish he'd seen in a long time.

"Mrs. Ross's brother?"

"It's all legal, Albert."

"I don't care if it isn't!"

"That's not like you! You're always banging on about them spivs making money instead of doing something proper for the war effort."

"Yeah, well, bad day. I'll tell you all about it on our walk. Got any vinegar?"

"No, Albert, I can't."

"What choice do we have? Champ's only two years old and look at him; crawling along exhausted and we've only been out fifteen minutes. It's no life for a young dog."

"You're just upset with what that bloke did to you. There's probably others that will be a bit kinder. Anyway, if I have a word with Mrs. Ross's brother maybe I can work out a deal with him to pass on anything he gets from gutting the fish he catches."

"It wouldn't keep Champ up if this war goes on much longer. A big dog like him, he needs meat."

"I know you're right, Albert, but... he's like my..."

"Don't cry, love. Come on, chin up, people will see."

"Who's going to see anything in this bloody blackout?"

Four weeks later Albert and Mabel were sitting in the vet's office with Champ between them.

"Well, I'd say he's still a reasonably healthy dog. Nothing organically wrong with him – nothing a bit more protein wouldn't sort out."

"Well, there's the problem in a nutshell, Doctor. Mabel's

been doing her best with whatever she can lay her hands on, but it's never enough."

"How did he get on with the vitamins I gave you?"

"He weren't that keen till Albert started putting them in Bovril sandwiches."

"Good, good. Well, I've thought a lot about your particular problem, Mr. And Mrs. Taylor, and I think that you've come to the right decision. I must say, I think it's very brave of you both."

"He won't suffer will he?"

"No, Mrs. Taylor, you have my word."

"What about after, what happens to him then?"

"When it's over the army will return him to you. I can assure you that he will be fed well, and get plenty of exercise. I hear that most of the dogs thoroughly enjoy the training."

Three years later, two months after the war ended, Albert was summoned to Waterloo Station to collect the property that had been voluntarily seconded to the army. He hadn't mentioned it to his wife. The surprise would do her good.

She'd not been the same since Champ left. It was like they'd sent their son off to war, except there were no letters, no leave, and no one to talk to about him. They didn't even know where he was.

A soldier handed Albert a lead with a fine-looking dog at the end of it. Champ looked very different from the scrawny, moth-eaten specimen that was offered to the army, which was wonderful, but he showed no sign of recognising Albert. He sat obediently, waiting for orders, no hint of movement in his tail.

On the bus ride and walk home Albert worried how Mabel would react to this new Champ. The dog walking by his side was a military animal, one that seemed only able to follow commands. With barely a tug on the lead Champ would stop, sit, stand, walk. Albert regretted that he hadn't asked the soldier whether Champ was safe to be a family pet again. Maybe he'd killed people.

Albert wished he had a piece of chocolate in his pocket, but at the same time thought about his old service pistol from the last war and the *Air Raid Precautions Handbook* with its horrible diagrams. He looked down at his dog and was glad that those pages had been flushed away.

Albert quietly opened his front door and Champ sedately walked into the hallway and sat.

"That you, Albert?"

Before he could answer, Champ gave a whine and ran into the kitchen where Mabel was making the tea. When Albert entered seconds later he saw his wife crying happily into the neck of her beloved dog. Champ was wagging his tail furiously, and peeing on the floor.

About the author
Helen Kreeger was born and raised in London, but has lived elsewhere for many years. She has been published in *Blunt Moms* (USA), *ARC 25, 26* and *27* (Israel), *Writing District,* (UK), *Café Aphra* (USA), *Scrittura Lit Mag* (UK), *Free Flash Fiction, With Painted Words* (UK), as well as being a contest runner-up in Striking 13, Creative Writing Ink, and Soundwork U.K.

Hello, I'm Listening

Marion Grace Woolley

If I tell you how it started, you'll think I'm an idiot. But you have no idea where I was at in my life back then, and it's not like I picked a message out of my spam telling me to send money to an account in Abuja. It felt like it was my decision. Something I had found for myself.

It was closer to February than December, and I was sitting in a freezing cold house, keeping myself warm with a bottle of Morgan Spice. The boiler had been on the blink ever since Kendra left, and that sort of felt righteous. You know, I'd driven her away, and all the warmth in the house left with her.

I fucking hated myself.

So, I booted up my laptop and started browsing. No direction or anything, just a half-hour of cartoons here, an hour of mukbang there, the ones where they put the microphone real close to the eater's mouth so you hear all those juicy, squelching sounds. I don't know, it's relaxing.

The screen just kept rolling, whatever the next video was, and I didn't have to think about it. I didn't have to think at all. Just sit there, in the dark and the Baltic cold, drinking, and drinking and drinking. Eventually, I passed out. Came to somewhere around 3 a.m. My throat was raw and my eyes half glued together with crusted salt.

I pushed the mouse and looked up my girlfriend's Facebook account. She'd blocked me. At the time, I thought it was torture, but I reckon she did it because she knew how much I'd suffer in the long run. Scrolling through every picture of her with another woman, driving myself crazy wondering whether she was sleeping with them or just posing. I guess it was a kindness, but it didn't feel like it

41

back then. I threw the empty bottle at the wall, the glass too thick to shatter, then spat at the screen.

Just about where my dribble stopped, I saw an advert. A mint-green logo on a white background. One of those Greek or Roman things, with a head facing in both directions. No title, just a caption: *Resolutions aren't just for New Year.*

It sounded corny as all hell, but I wiped the gob away with my sleeve and clicked on it. I've never cared that much for New Year, and I'd never made a resolution, so I'm not sure why it drew me in. Maybe because of that – because I'd never done it. Kendra leaving got me thinking about a whole world of things I'd never done. Never done and never said.

A swanky graphic rotated into view. The same logo, this time with the name *Resolutions* across the middle, followed by a few paragraphs of text:

It's never too late to make a change, to turn from your past and see a brighter future...

It sounded like a bunch of wank, so I scrolled past.

At the very bottom, it repeated the line about being able to make resolutions at any time of year, and underneath that was a button: *Make your resolution now.*

When I clicked it, a little box appeared with the words: *Stop drinking for twelve days.*

I glanced at the empty bottle by the skirting board. It's not like I was an alcoholic or anything, I was just going through a rough patch. But maybe it wouldn't hurt to rein it in a little. Besides, twelve days wasn't exactly a life sentence. I could manage that, right?

And I could. It was pretty tough. Much tougher than I thought. I physically moved all the remaining bottles into the garage so that I couldn't see them, but I did it. Not only that, sobriety brought with it a little kick of motivation, and

I finally called up the boilerman to come fix the fucking thing. After twelve days, I was back sitting in front of the computer, but this time warm and dry.

I'd forgotten all about the site, but a week later, the logo popped up on ads again and I thought, *hell, why not?* My first ever new-me resolution and I'd nailed it. This time, when I clicked the button, it said: *Do someone a favour.*

And what, top myself?

There wasn't anyone around to do a favour for. I ordered all my shopping online, I cooked at home, ate at home, watched movies at home. When was I ever going to bump into someone who needed my help? I chalked my earlier success up to beginner's luck and cracked open a can of Kaliber. My twelve days were up, but I wanted to see how long I could actually go without alcohol. Prolong my modest sense of achievement.

Two days later, the phone rang.

It was Allie. She'd just broken up with Sandra. There'd been fireworks to rival my own Devil's Night a couple of months earlier. She had nowhere to go and no one to turn to. Her parents stopped talking to her the day she moved in with her girlfriend, and her brother lived in Australia.

"Sure, come on over," I said.

I'd always fancied Allie. Who didn't? She had the whole emo thing going on. A sleek, black bouffant with purple extensions down either side, and this little pointed chin that made her seem more anime than human. Any other week, I might have tried to get her into bed, but my sense of alcohol-free saintdom told me, *no.* I was on the rebound and she was freshly wounded. We were both grieving, and that was not the type of comfort required.

"You know," she said, as she packed her bag on the fifth day. "I always really liked you, Tams. You know that, right? You're a really good friend."

43

She kissed me on the cheek as she walked out the door. Her brother had wired her the money to visit, and she'd leapt at the chance to fly as far away as possible.

I felt kind of good about myself. Glowy. You know, it made me think perhaps I wasn't the streak of shit I'd started to believe I was. I'd actually done something kind and altruistic for a friend. Hadn't asked anything in return.

So, it was that evening I went back to the site. Two good things had come of it, one after the other, and good things always come in threes.

I hit the button again every couple of weeks. Within two months, I'd cleared out my closet and given everything I didn't need to charity, quit eating meat to become a pescatarian, started walking my elderly neighbour's dog once a day and began volunteering at the Red Cross. Twice a week, I'd stand in the basement of the building, steaming donated clothes and sorting children's toys into those we could sell and those we needed to burn. Seriously, there were some creepy home-knitted, button-eyed abominations in there.

And then, things went sideways.

I sat down at the beginning of May and clicked the button for my next self-improvement task. Instead, I got: *Take a vacation to a foreign land.*

Yeah, great. I was living off benefits, and the occasional book cover design I hawked online. Kendra had been the breadwinner in our relationship, and I had just enough money to pay rent each month. There was no way I was jetting off to the Bahamas any time soon.

I felt an irrational flush of anger. Perhaps disappointment. I'd really come to rely on that site. Whenever I was at my lowest, starting to get self-critical and down, it threw me a lifeline. Gave me something manageable to focus on, and a warm sense of achievement once I'd finished. But I was just another social-media junkie, and this was my drug of choice. Of course that website didn't *know* me. Well, not beyond what Facebook had sold of me. It wasn't an actual friend, we didn't have conversations about my inner personal life, and it never WhatsApped to check on me. It was just a stupid random task generator. All algorithms and anagnorisis. The sudden reveal that, beneath my sorry ass, there might just be the beating heart of a half-decent human being.

What a shocker.

And now it was throwing me this shit. *Go on holiday*, it said. Might as well have read, *win the bloody lottery*. Instead of lifting me up and giving me confidence, it just reminded me of all the things I couldn't do.

I closed the screen and cleared my browsing history. The URL was a long one and I knew I'd forget it in a few days. I went downstairs to the garage and returned with a bottle of merlot. I'd probably keep walking Mrs Dougherty's dog, but in the morning I was going to call up the Red Cross and quit, then cook myself a full English with sausages, bacon and black pudding.

A week went by, then two. Pretty soon, I'd forgotten all about the website and returned to my usual routine of cyberstalking and heavy drinking. That little spark of soul had gone out, and the future once again looked bleak. Each morning the post came: a dole check, several bills, and another reminder for a smear test. I built a little bonfire in the garden and waited for them to cut off the phone line.

Then, one day, I clawed out from between my covers to find a bright-red envelope on the mat. It felt as thick as a birthday card, but it wasn't my birthday. When I opened it, I just stared for an age. It was a ticket to Zanzibar, an island off the coast of Tanzania. With the ticket came a set of instructions, including a boat ride to a private island called Kisiwa cha Uchawi.

I thought about it for three days. Right up until the point my boiler cut out again. It was the craziest thing I'd ever done in my life. I hadn't been on a plane since I was twenty, when we went on a hen do for Emma's wedding and hired one of those beer bars you cycle around the streets of Prague. Sitting there, freezing cold and out of wine, I realised that my passport was still in date. I saw my future a month down the line. Still sitting there, still shivering my tits off, and glaring at a phone that never rang.

Or I could be lying on a beach somewhere, sipping margaritas.

When I stepped off the plane in Africa, I almost melted to the tarmac. The trip had been chronically unpleasant. Taking off my shoes and belt to go through security, my sticky feet padding over tiles no doubt crawling with verrucas. Cramped seats, headphones that crackled like cellophane, and food you had to hold your nose to swallow. But the boat ride to the island was utterly incredible. I didn't know the sea could lie so still, like an azure blanket threaded with silver. We even saw dolphins. Three of them, racing ahead of the boat, leaping and laughing.

Of course, I wondered about it. I knew people didn't give away holidays like this for nothing. I knew someone had been watching me and waiting. Someone connected to that website. And yes, underneath that calm ocean was a cold current of uncertainty. But I was living the moment. It was the first time in months that my day had not been completely predictable. I didn't know what I'd have to eat that night or where I would sleep. If it was all some elaborate con, I'd figure it out when I got there.

But, oh! The island. It was straight out of a holiday brochure. A lush, green emerald embedded in the Indian Ocean. A seamless band of gold beach. If you had asked me to close my eyes and imagine paradise – this was it.

I checked into the little guesthouse as instructed, though I did change rooms. If some creep had set this whole thing up, they'd have to work to find me in the night. Unless, I suppose, they knew the receptionist… which was likely. I pushed such thoughts to the very back of my mind and focussed on the crystal-clear swimming pool and the ocean view. There was even a bowl of fruit: pineapples, mangos, passion fruit, and a shiny red thing that looked like a misshapen tomato.

Within a week, I was perfectly at home.

Within three weeks, I had already decided I wasn't going back.

Why should I? Go back to what? In the time I'd been there, I'd designed ten book covers and sold eight. The room was paid up for another week, and the landlady could give me a monthly price for less than I was paying in the UK. I could sublet my old rental and live off the income from that. If I ever changed my mind, it was just a half-day flight back to the grey misery of Maidenhead.

I once tried to ask the receptionist who had originally paid, but she gave me a funny look and said, "You did." I didn't press further in case she got suspicious and realised there'd been some mistake.

I'd spent the entire day reading on the beach with rum punch, served in an actual coconut. The inside of the guesthouse felt like a soothing balm after the heat of the sun. I removed my shades as I headed for the stairs.

"—without her. I mean, what am I supposed to do? There won't be another ferry until next week at the earliest."

I turned back to look at a large Tanzanian guy dressed like the Man from Del Monte. His jacket visibly strained at the gut and a thin sheen of sweat coated his brow. He dabbed it away with his handkerchief.

"If I could help, then I would," the receptionist was telling him. "But you see me here, I have a business to run."

She was about to say more, when they both became aware of my presence.

"Sorry," I said. "I shouldn't have been listening."

I turned to scuttle up the steps.

"No, wait!" the receptionist called out.

Reluctantly, I approached the counter.

"Miss Tamara, this is my good friend Mr Shabani."

The man held out his hand, which completely enveloped my own. He shook effusively and smiled.

"He has a problem," the receptionist explained. "Perhaps you can help him with it, since you're practically a local?"

"It's the telephones," he said, as though that was all the explanation needed.

"The telephones?" I repeated, slowly.

"Reginald here runs an outsourcing business on the island. One of his interns has amoebas and needed to see a doctor on the mainland. There aren't enough people to answer his phones."

"They need good English," Mr Shabani said, looking at me with hope in his eyes. "It would only be for a couple of weeks."

I wanted to say no. I was perfectly happy lazing my days away by the pool and drinking coconut juice, but instead, I found myself shrugging and smiling. Why not? Besides, I liked the way the receptionist had said I was local. Though I felt a twinge of shame that she knew my name and I didn't know hers.

It was settled.

The next day, I walked in the early morning mist, down the sand-covered path to Mr Shabani's office. It was a large, white building with a spacious room that opened at the back

48

onto a really pretty garden, all banana fronds and pineapple trees. Twelve desks were arranged, back-to-back, so they formed two rows of six with a half-hearted attempt to partition them with plywood. This had slid down between the desks so that you could clearly see the person in front of you. Not that anyone else was there.

"Ah, you came," Mr Shabani said, appearing in the garden doorway. "*Karibu, karibu*, come, take a seat."

He gestured to the chair I was standing in front of, and I sat down.

The job was simple. I was to sit at the desk and answer calls until relief arrived at 8 p.m. The difficult part was that this wasn't a sales job. It was a little more like the Samaritans. Outsourcing psychological help to whoever cried out for it.

"Don't I need some sort of training for this?" I asked, after he'd explained for the second time how the switchboard worked.

"Not really," he replied. "Most people who break down, do so in the late hours. Something about the absence of light draws the sadness from them. The calls you will receive should be manageable. Simply build a rapport and refer them to one of the numbers on this list, see – drug addiction, suicide, self-harm, and so forth."

"But, if people are calling in from everywhere in the world, it must be night somewhere?"

He simply grunted and drew a handkerchief from his pocket to wipe his brow. The day was becoming humid, and I wished that I'd gone to the beach instead.

"You'll do fine. I'll be in my office if you need me."

He walked out of the room and left me alone with the telephone.

It didn't ring for over an hour.

When it did, I dropped my game of Candy Crush and sat to attention.

"Hello, Soul to Soul, I'm listening."

"Hi." A faint voice came on the line.

"Hi," I replied.

The story was terribly sad. A girl who was gay, like me. Her parents had thrown her out; her girlfriend had broken up with her. Her brother let her visit, but she didn't fit in with his family. His wife hated her, and she couldn't sleep because their baby kept crying at night. She didn't know where to go or what to do. She'd tried to call a friend, but the friend wasn't picking up. Her voice sounded familiar, as though she was someone I might once have known, but I couldn't remember her name.

"Don't worry," I said. "Let me know which area you're in and I'll give you all the details for housing support and a local LGBT group. You're going to be just fine."

"Thank you," she said.

I felt much better when we hung up. She'd sounded brighter, more hopeful.

The next call was from a woman with a thick Estuary accent. She ran a charity shop, but all her volunteers kept leaving and she was depressed because she was starting to feel that she would never be able to form a meaningful relationship with any of them. She wasn't married, didn't have children, and spent all her time at the shop. The constant change of faces was making her feel like everyone else had somewhere to be except her. As though life was something that happened to other people and she was just standing there, behind the counter, waiting for it to end. I asked about her hobbies and put her in contact with some social groups in her area.

I was starting to feel good about this job, when the third call came.

I knew the voice on the other end instantly.

My throat tightened and I stared ahead at the garden.

It was growing darker out there, the evening shadows reaching like fingers towards the door. My voice came out husky, which is probably why she didn't recognise me. But, as I listened to Kendra whispering softly down the line, I felt as though I was right there with her, our foreheads touched together on the pillow.

"I loved her so much," she said. "We had known each other for so long, and I thought we would know each other always. I still can't figure out how it all went so wrong."

"Have you tried calling her?" I managed. "Have you tried telling her that?"

"Yes, but she never picks up. I know she'll never pick up again."

I let out a stinted laugh. That was so ridiculous. What was she talking about?

"Kendra," I said, tears rolling down my cheeks. "Kendra, don't you recognise my voice? It's me. It's Tams."

Only the dial tone replied.

When I glanced up, there was Mr Shabani leaning against the wall, his big, dark eyes holding mine on a leash.

"What's going on?" I asked, slowly replacing the receiver. "What kind of place is this, really?"

"Welcome to Resolutions," he replied.

"You're the website I've been using? You sent me the tickets?"

"You never left your room."

"What? Don't be ridiculous. I got on a plane to come here. There was a boat."

"Still, it's a little cool for the tropics, don't you think?"

I glanced at the garden, where the evening sun folded across verdigris lawns and thick vegetation. Yet, I knew what he meant. The heat didn't reach inside, and the hairs on my skin prickled. It felt chilly, as though the boiler had gone out.

51

The phone rang, causing me to jump.

"Hello," I answered. "Soul to Soul, I'm listening."

"Hello."

It was my own voice.

I looked up at Reginald, and he nodded for me to go on, but before I could find my voice, the one on the other end spoke first.

"I think I need help," it said.

My entire body ached, a dam holding back the impending flood.

"I know," I said softly.

"I think it might already be too late."

"Yes."

"It's Kendra, you see – she's gone. And the heating won't stay on. I can't get warm since she left. I think I'm drinking too much. Like, a lot too much. I just can't seem to get my head on straight."

I couldn't do it.

I couldn't reply.

Slowly, I hung up on myself. Part of my mind couldn't comprehend what was happening, and the other part understood all too well.

"Kendra didn't leave, did she?"

"No," Reginald replied.

"But I did?"

He simply nodded.

"So, what is this place supposed to be, heaven?"

"More of a halfway house."

"Between life and death?"

"Between who you were and who you want to be."

I fucking hated riddles, why didn't everybody just speak plainly?

"Wait," I said. "I can't be dead. What about Allie? She came to visit me after Kendra left – after I left. Whatever.

She was there, in my house. She was real. She stayed for five days."

"And what did you do in those five days?"

"All sorts of stuff. We—" I paused for a moment, thinking. What had we done in those five days? I remembered her being there, we must have done something. "I don't know. I guess we watched telly? But she couldn't have been there unless we were both alive. Or unless we were both…"

"Go on."

"Unless we were both dead?"

I didn't like the smile on Reginald's face.

"That phoneline is for the living," he said. "They call in their dreams to express their pain. They want to be heard, to make sense of all the confusion."

"So, it really was Allie who called, and she's alive?"

"Yes. She made a full recovery."

"She tried to kill herself after she split up with Sandra, and that's when she was with me? Then she tried to call me, and I didn't pick up because I was – I am dead?"

"You're deciding."

"Deciding what?"

"Whether to be dead or not."

"What do you mean?"

"Usually, suicides are pretty certain. They spend a day or two moping around their homes. We knock on the door, they realise what's happened, accept what they've done, and follow us into the light. You were a little different. You moped about for a couple of months, you ignored every knock at the door, then you found our website. You only find Resolutions if you're looking to make a change in yourself. You got your boiler fixed, quit drinking, became a pescatarian, helped a friend out, and started volunteering at a charity shop. People who have completely given up on this world, don't tend to do that."

"Fuck."

I fully admit, that wasn't the most elegant response I could have given, but it was all I was capable of.

"So," I said, staring at the phone. "What happens now?"

"One of three choices. You can switch off the light altogether. Become nothing, lose your consciousness forever. Hardly anyone chooses that."

"No," I agreed. "That does sound rather final."

"Then you have two options. Either return to being who you were or become someone else."

"Reincarnation?"

"That's the standard. Pick one of the jungle paths and start walking. With each step, you'll forget a little more of who you once were, and eventually you'll wake screaming in a hospital bed somewhere in the world. Maybe a boy, maybe a girl—"

"Can I still be gay?"

"You don't get to choose."

I looked disappointed.

"How far in the future will I be born?"

"That depends how long the path is. It's different for everyone."

"And the other option?"

"Return to your body."

"Well, what kind of state is it in? I mean, what did I do to myself?"

Reginald looked over his shoulder, down the corridor, then back.

"It's not too bad. Pills, so no visible scars."

"Is Kendra there?" I asked.

"Yes."

This left me very quiet. The thought of her sitting by my

bedside, waiting for me to wake up. It really floored me. I didn't care about myself anymore, but what had I done to her?

"Is she asleep?" I asked.

When he nodded, I picked up the phone and dialled her number.

"Hello?" a sleepy voice on the other end.

"Hi, Kendra. It's me, Tams."

"Tams?" her voice sounded strained, but happy.

"Yeah. I just wanted to check in. Let you know I'm doing fine. I'm in a good place."

"God, I've missed you. What the hell were you thinking?"

"I don't know."

"Was it that stupid row? Were you angry at me? Did you do this just to spite me?"

"What row?"

"You don't remember?"

"I don't remember any of it. Only how much I love you. How happy I am that we met. How happy I am that you were mine."

She began to cry, but I tried hard not to.

"I never meant to hurt you," she says. "It was a silly thing, just one drunken night."

"I know," I reply. "And it wasn't you, I promise. Don't have that thought anymore when you wake. It was just me. Something about me. I just wasn't meant to stay. It's like those bricks that kids play with, y'know? I just always felt like a square peg in a round hole. I didn't fit. Maybe next time, though."

"Please don't go."

"I won't go yet."

I began to sing to her. A silly song about high heels and tiaras that we used to listen to down the club when we first met. It always made her laugh, and I'd break into it to try and stop an argument, which sometimes worked. She didn't sing along, she just listened, and I repeated the last verse twice, so that we'd have a little more time.

When I hung up, I cried like a child.

"You've made up your mind, then?" Reginald said, when I finally quieted.

"Yeah, I have."

"Is there anyone else you'd like to call?"

"No."

He came over and took me by the hand, leading me out to the garden. At the end of the perfectly manicured lawn, the jungle rose up, deep and dark, and dancing with brightly coloured birds and the maraca call of cicadas.

"Just start walking," he said. "After a while, the path will fork. Take whichever direction you fancy."

"Thanks," I replied, still sore with loss.

The jungle looked utterly impenetrable; sweating and breathing like a living body.

"Hey," he said, as I took my first step. "Why didn't you want to go back?"

I found it hard to answer, but I tried.

"All those good things I did after I found your site, they were just patching up mistakes I'd been making all my life. If I went back, I'd constantly feel like I was trying to pay off a debt, reparation for all the bad things I'd done. Running to catch that bus you can never get on. And everyone around me, treading on eggshells, worried what I might do next, eating away at their own peace of mind until they wound up famished. Some things, you just can't make right. But I've learnt from it, and I want to try again. Not a resolution once a year, but once a lifetime. There's so much I want to do better next time. So many things I want to change."

56

"Well," said Reginald. "Let me know how that goes next time I see you."

"I will," I said, with a smile.

One step, and I forgot the colour of my parents' front door. Two steps, and I forgot that I ever had a childhood pet. Three steps, and I forgot the name of my best friend at school. Four steps, and I forgot where I met Kendra.

Five steps, and I forgot my name.

About the author

Marion is a British author based in Rwanda. She first moved to the country as a sign language researcher in 2007, and later returned to start a consultancy helping to support non-profit organisations working in human rights and economic development. She tends towards the darker side of fiction and has penned several novels including *Those Rosy Hours at Mazandaran*, *The Children of Lir* and *Secure the Shadow*. She was shortlisted for the Luke Bitmead Bursary for New Writers in 2009 and won the Bet Tuppi's Near Eastern Historical Fiction Prize in 2021. As well as writing fiction, Marion has also taught it as a lecturer with the University of Global Health Equity. In her spare time, she fixes broken pianos and acts as servant and subordinate to her three cats.

I Resolve to Die at Sixty-five

Hannah Retallick

December 31st – 07:00

It is my final day of being sixty-five and the final day of my life.

It was my fortieth birthday, Dec 31st, 1995, when I jotted down the words: *I Resolve to Die at Sixty-five*. That journal is open beside me. I never wrote why I made the decision, as it was not something I would forget, and it seemed crude to put it into words; her illness was too raw. How does one come to terms with their mother's sudden deterioration? One can only try to avoid the same fate.

I do not know how my death will come to pass. 'Come to pass', an intriguing expression with a biblical quality. 'Come to pass away' is better still; it is less exact than 'I do not know how I will die' but involves a delightful play on words. I am not sure how I will come to pass away.

I have not determined the time of my death either. This, coupled with the above paragraph, is a thorn in my side, a barbed wire, a knife to my heart, a bunch of stinging nettles dragged across my bare stomach. I must clarify that my stomach is not, at present, bare – simply that it would have to be bare for the analogy to work. Upon reflection, the thorn-in-my-side metaphor is, although an overused expression, the most accurate in this instance.

The years have 'gone in a flash'. What an ugly phrase. There is something in the sentiment, however. The years line my walls – blue journals for the first five and a half, and green journals for the rest, due to a misguided decision by WHSmith.

It is time for my 07:15 coffee. I shall have it with four

lumps of sugar instead of three, seeing as it is my deathday.

11:00

I do not know how to recount the morning. It started in a normal way, when I read the weather forecast and stepped out into the porch to see whether the world agreed with the BBC. It did, for once: sunny intervals and a moderate breeze. Happy deathday, Gordon.

However, I soon received confirmation that I ought not to let my life extend beyond sixty-five years. The breeze turned immoderate. That was the first thing the woman said, though not in those words – she did not seem the sort of person to use the word 'immoderate'. Her attire suggested shop work of some kind. I do not mean this in a disparaging way.

What matter? The clock. Too much thinking; too little writing.

I must be resolute.

15:00

The day is fast diminishing. My to-do list is insignificant, but I am still at a loss regarding the time and method of my death – the only activity in CAPITALS. Activity. I'm not sure that is the right expression; it reeks of clay pottery and juvenile ball games.

Perhaps the decades will drown me, bury me, smash my head to smithereens. Perhaps it could happen naturally, or someone could be persuaded to come here and fight me, causing the bookcase to fall, like in… that novel. Oh, Gordon, which novel? It will come to me. All that comes to me now is her next words.

"Warm out, isn't it?"

I am no expert in the field of temperature, but I believed it to be no more than six degrees Celsius, a calculation that was confirmed by the thermometer as soon as I returned home. I hardly consider this to be warm, especially when combined with an immoderate breeze. Perhaps she had meant it was warm for the season, or that, due to her heavy coat with a furry lining in the hood, it seemed warmer than it was.

It is only now I realise she was probably joking. It seems in keeping with her charming, jovial persona. It has been a long time since someone has attempted to engage with me humorously, and I must say, it was rather agreeable.

19:00

I have been obsessing over the bookcase death, and the name of its victim. I believe it starts with B. Something B. Which book though? Come on, Gordon, you can do better than this. I must never surrender to Google. I have no doubts about that woman and her use of Google, Facebook, and whatever else is currently poisoning mankind. She had her phone in her hand the whole time she was at the bus stop, flicking her thumbs up and down. It didn't stop her talking though. The conservation gradually comes back to me.

"Where are you off to?"

Did she want to know the location or the purpose of my excursion?

"Coffee."

She nodded, more thumb flicking, and then a smile. "You meeting someone?"

"I am not."

It seems an odd thing to ask a person. It implies that they are not complete unless they are in the presence of another party – an implication I believe to be both incorrect and insulting. However, I chose not to contradict her.

"Have you made any New Year's resolutions?" she asked.

I hesitated momentarily.

"I haven't," she continued. "It's best to just live your life, isn't it?"

"Certainly," I said.

I must cease these foolish recollections and make dinner now. As it is Tuesday, I should be eating spaghetti bolognaise for my last supper, but I have a craving for baked beans on toast, and I'm in the mood to indulge myself.

23:00 (Late – 23:22)

Most pleasant aspect of the day: a nice woman spoke to me, under no obligation.

Most unpleasant aspect of the day: forgetting which book included the bookcase death.

Observation of the day: pain can be more intense as an onlooker.

Mother had barely seemed to notice her sixty-six-year-old mind becoming more like a ninety-year-old's, but it impacted me greatly. However, I have no children to grieve for me. So, if I do not notice my own deterioration, what does it matter?

I consider this further, accompanied by my 23:15 hot chocolate. A glance at the clock had informed me that it was already 23:17, but given recent developments, I went ahead with the journal session and hot chocolate anyway.

Mother used to tell me I was far too obsessed with schedules and finer details – I expect the lady today would view things similarly. Controlling, inflexible, Mother would say. I do not agree. I like things to be in order, yes. Life is chaotic and confusing; who would not want to simplify it as much as possible? It is why I favour books. They hint at life's complexities whilst containing them within neat, tidy blocks. (Oh, which had the bookcase death? I shall probably remember as I am trying to sleep.)

It is strange to write with my drink beside me. I look up occasionally and touch the side of the mug with my fingertips, to ascertain the temperature, as I should not like it to become cold. You may be surprised that, despite the allotted time having long-since passed, I am in no rush to finish writing in my journal – not as surprised as I.

I doubt she keeps a journal; she is the sort of free spirit who would prefer to go out with friends, swinging her wavy red hair, even at that stage of life. I should guess forty, the same age I was when I decided, or a year or two above. The area around her eyes wrinkled when she smiled, which was often, but when it fell to a neutral position the skin was somewhat smooth. Although it is unlikely that we shall meet again, I would like to know who she is. I believe her badge said 'Angelica' – aside from the Yellow Pages, my ability to find her is limited. This, admittedly, is one of the few benefits of websites such as Facebook.

My last statement is evidence that I should be in bed, asleep, safe from these strangely pleasant, warm thoughts. There are other things I would like to communicate, and it is a source of frustration to me that, despite these sensations being some of the strongest I've experienced in a long time, I am struggling to put them into words. They are like vivid dreams that fade when you wake and leave only feelings. Perhaps this is what it means when people describe themselves as 'only human': willing to forsake reason sometimes and not overanalyse their emotions.

23:59

As Angelica said, "It's best to just live your life."

I shall never again make a resolution.

January 1st – 03:22

Howard's End by EM Forster! The tragic death of Leonard Bast. Upon reflection, it would be an extremely unpleasant way to go.

About the author

Hannah Retallick is from Anglesey, North Wales. She was home-educated and then studied with the Open University, graduating with a First-class honours degree, BA in Humanities with Creative Writing and Music, before passing her Creative Writing MA with a Distinction. She was shortlisted in the Writing Awards at the Scottish Mental Health Arts Festival 2019, the Cambridge Short Story Prize, the Henshaw Short Story Competition June 2019, the Bedford International Writing Competition 2019, the Crossing the Tees book festival competition 2020, and the Fish Publishing Short Story Prize 2021.

https://www.hannahretallick.co.uk/

Jump

Karissa Venne

Target was quiet at 7 in the morning. Almost serene. Almost as if it wasn't really open.

Felicity was walking from department to department – from shoes to home goods to furniture – and the only other people she'd seen were two Target employees, their red polos wrinkled and tucked into khakis, and an old lady in bright pink leggings pushing a cart heaped high with bags of cat food.

Felicity did not have a cart. She didn't even have a basket. She hadn't collected a single item.

Felicity couldn't remember the last time she'd wandered a store without a list, without a purpose, without a jug of laundry detergent tucked under her arm, a bag of onions hanging from her hand, a package of 5-blade razors grasped in the other.

There was always something that they needed: gallon-size freezer bags, hand soap for the kitchen, AA batteries for the smoke detectors and the vibrators. That was what adulthood was, an endless parade of basic needs. This would only get worse, Felicity realised, as she considered last night.

She circled the store in a daze, her flip flops thwacking against the tile floor. In front of the women's clothing section, two mannequins in swimsuits greeted her, their hands resting on their hips and their bikinis revealing pearly flat stomachs. One wore a floppy straw hat that looked too big for its plastic head. Felicity stared at their featureless faces, a jolt of emotion flapping in her chest. It took her a moment to recognise the feeling for what it was. Jealousy. She was jealous of these mannequins and their freedom, their make-believe beach day.

It took all of three minutes for Felicity to realise that she could do whatever she wanted, that she was a person with an open day, that she'd left her wife in bed that morning without even a 'Gone to the store' message scribbled on a piece of paper, that she had nowhere to be.

She was a shopper with a plan now.

Her body surged with energy, as if she'd shot an espresso. Rifling through the racks, she chose a black bikini in what she hoped was her size, the mannequins staring down at her with gleaming approval. Circling the store again, her flip flops slapped much louder against the floor. She marched from section to section, grabbing a bottle of sunblock, a small cooler, a book, a towel, and a beach chair. After checking out, she slipped the bikini on in the Target bathroom.

After stopping at the deli next door to buy a sandwich, chips, a bag of ice, and a twist-off bottle of rosé, Felicity threw her wares into the trunk. She texted Veronica, who was probably up by now and worried. Three dots popped up, but Felicity turned her phone off before Veronica's response could appear. With a pang she realised that without her phone, there would be no Google Maps, no robotic female voice directing her way. She'd drive north. Maine was north. The highway signs would lead her there. It would be an adventure in so many ways.

Three hours and four CDs later, the beach signs began to appear, sprouting from the side of the highway like tall, hopeful flowers. She picked one – Crescent Beach – and followed the signs that led her off of I-95, then left, right, right, left, right, and she was there.

She passed a $20 to a pimply teen at the entrance, parked, and unloaded her supplies. The sand was already searing. It burned the bottoms of Felicity's feet as she weaved through the blankets, her chair's strap digging into her shoulder. The cooler hung from her hand, dripping water across the sand.

She unfolded her chair alongside a small outcropping of rocks with a front row seat to the glittering, dark blue Maine ocean. The chair's price tag flew in the wind like a flag of surrender. Easing into her seat, she plucked the fresh bottle of sunblock from her bag and applied it.

She couldn't remember the last time she had been to the beach alone. In fact, had she ever? She and Veronica beached every summer, or at least they used to. They'd rent a cottage in Maine with their golden, Puck, and spend every moment of daylight on the beach. Packing half of the fridge in their cooler, they'd sprawl out with a pack of cards and a stack of paperbacks. They gulped down cold brew coffees in the mornings, guzzled iced teas in the afternoons, and sipped gin and tonics in the evenings. They'd wade into the ocean, Puck waiting for them on the shore, their fingers laced together to jump the waves.

But she had never come alone.

She slid the paperback that everyone had read last summer from her bag. She began to peel the price tag from its front cover, then thought better of it. There was something about leaving the price tag intact, the oversized circle with '30% off' in bold red letters – a glaring bullseye – that said: this book is new, this day is new, I can have a new life, if only for today.

Looking up in between chapters, she watched a group of twenty-something women arrive and set up three blankets in a row in front of her. They sprawled out, each with a book in hand, and passed cans of wine from one end of the blankets to the other.

Wine in cans. Why didn't Felicity think of that? She grimaced at the image of her just-bought bottle of twist-off rosé in her cooler, at her plan to rinse out her already used plastic coffee cup. But cans of wine?

Felicity knew she sounded about a hundred years old, not her mere thirty-two. But when was it that she had stopped reading a book a week, stopped knowing to buy cans of wine for the beach, stopped doing things just for the fun of them? Actually, she knew exactly when she'd stopped, but she wasn't thinking about that.

Felicity remembered her twenties as an ocean of tears, filled with hopes for her thirties: In her thirties, she'd save more money. In her thirties, she'd floss more. In her thirties, she'd quit waking up hungover so often. In her thirties, she'd get it together and all of this misery would be a pale memory. What she didn't factor in was what Veronica would want her thirties to be. And there lay the crux of the problem. The immovable boulder that Felicity was not moving today.

It was warm for early June. Felicity removed her shirt and adjusted her black bikini top, only then remembering to rip the tag from its strap. She listened to the caw of seagulls overhead, the crash of waves on the beach in front of her, the cacophony of music happening all around her. To her left, hip hop blared. Behind her, country crooned. Indie hummed from the canned-wine group. Veronica would have loved it.

The beach was crowded now. Umbrellas dotted the sand. Beach-dwellers unwrapped sandwiches, tore open bags of chips, reapplied sunscreen to their kids' faces. A group of men flung a frisbee. A woman jogged by the shore, weaving through the crowd, sweat rolling down her body. Kids boogie-boarded in the water with strands of hair plastered to their faces.

Of course there were kids here. Felicity hadn't considered that possibility when she'd decided to come. They were all the same: wearing bright swimsuits, covered in sand, their wet hair dripping.

67

There were toddlers, too. Waddling toddlers with bonnets and floaties led to the water by their parents' hands, coos of praise echoing down the shore.

And then the babies. Felicity knew they were there even if she couldn't see them. They were in those strollers and carriers, light blankets floating over them, parents peeking underneath every few minutes because what if they were too hot? Getting too much sun? Was bringing them to the beach even safe?

Babies. Felicity would gladly run the length of this beach naked to never hear the word 'baby' again, to throw it against those rocks and hear it shatter into letters.

To erase every baby she'd watched Veronica drool over for the past two years.

To forget about the intense savings plan they'd concocted six months ago, as IUI and sperm donors weren't cheap.

To remove the day last week when they found out Veronica's hormonal levels were low.

And then, last night. Veronica's pitch: They'd sell their house, downsize to a cheap apartment, and commit to IVF, the priciest of fertility options.

As Veronica begged, Felicity looked around at the small old house they'd saved for, that she'd thought they both loved. Its scratched hardwood floors and its tall windows. The built-in hutch in the kitchen. The laundry chute in the bathroom. The front porch with its about-to-break third step.

A stony pit formed in her stomach. She watched the tears gather in Veronica's eyes as she told Felicity yet again about how being a mother was her life's ambition, that she couldn't live without a child, that her life, her life with Felicity, wasn't worth living if there wasn't another person added to it. And Felicity, for the thousandth time, swallowed her dread, her deep unwanting, her very soul, and said, "Okay."

When had she become this person? Someone small and quiet? Someone who had let her wife's dreams eclipse her own? Wasn't aging supposed to make you stronger, wiser, smarter, more self-assured?

Twenty-two year old Felicity, standing in a bar with a vodka soda sweating in her hand while a twenty-five-year-old Veronica belted "Come to my Window," her glitter eyeshadow sparkling despite the dim bar lights, *that* Felicity never would have stood for this. That Felicity knew who she was, what she wanted. Didn't she prove it that night ten years ago when she asked Veronica to come home with her?

Felicity twisted the cap from her wine and began drinking straight from the bottle. She'd forgotten what rosé tasted like. Like freedom.

The afternoon stretched on, the sun beating its white hot rays on the beach-goers' skin. People napped, baseball caps balancing precariously on their faces to block out the sun from their eyes. Felicity's sandwich was long gone; she was now demolishing the bag of chips, streaking grease on the book's pages. Sweat dripped down her stomach. Swimming sounded appealing, but she couldn't imagine leaving her book.

The tide came in. Some families departed, their kids tired and sunburnt. The wine can girls were all sleeping now. Felicity watched as a group of teenagers considered climbing the outcropping of rocks. The leader, a boy in a baseball cap and blue swim trunks, searched for the easiest route up and heaved his body to the top. Three more boys and one girl followed. They carefully made their way to the edge, the ocean spread wide below them, waves crashing against the rocks beneath their bare feet. Felicity didn't know what was going to happen until it did: the leader jumped.

Felicity worried that it was too shallow, that the boy had made a fatal error, but he bobbed up to the surface just fine, grinning with his hat still in place. She kept watching, finishing the last gulps of her wine and using her finger as a bookmark, as the other three boys leapt from the rock into the water, each one getting more height than the last.

Only the girl was left. She tiptoed to the edge of the rock and peered over, her arms crossed tight around her stomach. The boys cheered for her and shouted tips like, "Bend your knees!" or "Back up and run for it!" but she didn't budge. Desperately, she scanned the scene for an escape. A ladder maybe, or some steps carved perfectly from rock. Five minutes, ten minutes.

Just jump already, Felicity wanted to yell. Be braver than this. The boys didn't think, didn't pause. You did and you let all of your doubts and fears slip onto your skin like wet sand.

But she was still stuck. The boys were becoming bored now. They waited in the water, floating and splashing each other, occasionally yelling half-hearted encouragement. One trudged back to the beach, yelling, "She'll never do it!" to the friends he'd left behind. The girl stared at the water, fists clenched at her sides, her chest heaving with scared breaths. Felicity felt like she was going to explode watching her. Why didn't she jump already?

Finally, the girl unclenched her fists, squeezed her eyes shut, and leapt. She soared even higher than the boys, the tiny thing that she was. The boys whooped and cheered. The spectators on the beach clapped.

Felicity didn't clap. She didn't cheer. There was a roaring frustration in her chest, a light-headed panic starting up in her head. Though the girl was now bobbing in the water, all Felicity could see was her soaring.

She gathered her possessions, hurried to her car, and drove the three hours home. It was silent except for the huffing of the air conditioner.

When Felicity arrived, Puck greeted her at the door.

Veronica was sitting at the kitchen table with a formidable stack of papers to grade planted in front of her. Evening summer light painted lines across their kitchen. There was a half-eaten banana by Veronica's hand, a glass of tap water sweating beside it. The ceiling fan clicked as it spun above them.

Felicity dropped her things at the door, sand spilling onto the kitchen tile. Veronica squinted at her. "Where have you…"

Felicity interrupted her. "I…"

"I texted you like twelve different times. Did your phone die?"

Felicity swallowed and started again.

"I went…"

"You really scared me, you know."

Felicity remembered the girl, suspended in air.

Then, she said it.

"I don't want a baby."

Saying it was like leaping off of a rock and plunging into the bright and cold sea.

About the author

Karissa Venne is a writer who lives in Western Massachusetts with her soon-to-be wife and their epileptic kitten. She received her MFA from The New School and works as a Digital Resource Development Editor at Oxford University Press. Her work has appeared or is forthcoming in *Okay Donkey*, *Sonder*, and *F(r)iction*. Find her online at @kvenne717 and https://karissavenne.com.

Marta's Bread

Liz Cox

The stranger was kneeling beside her sister's still body when Marta arrived outside her home. He looked up at her and shook his head. All around there was rubble and dust. Cowering amongst the fractured stones, she saw her nephew, Karim, and his younger sister, Elena. Their faces were streaked with dirt and tears; their white school shirts dyed by the red dust from the street and the blood of their mother. The smell of burning and sulphur hung in the air.

"I'm sorry, there was nothing I could do." The man was apologising, but Marta could not hear him. As she bent down to touch her sister, the man laid a gentle hand on Marta's shoulder then moved quietly away leaving her to her sorrow.

"Sleep tight, my sister," she whispered as she touched Anna's bloody face and stroked her matted hair; fair where her own was dark. She had always been jealous of Anna's blonde hair, but now it was plastered to her sister's shattered skull, dark with drying blood. She clenched her fists and rounded on the assembled crowd; she could feel the fury shining from her eyes.

"How can we let this happen?" she shouted to no one in particular. The babbling crowd was silent and then one by one they slunk away into the rubble of the bombed-out building. They had no answer for her. Tears filled her eyes, as she wrapped Anna's shredded green skirt closely around what was left of her body, while she waited for the rescuers to take her older sister's corpse away. The bomb had hit Anna straight on as she returned from picking the children up from school. She was a mangled mess of blood and bone. Impatiently, Marta rubbed angry tears from her face

72

leaving dusty, bloody streaks down her cheeks and turned towards the children.

"Come with me, my darlings. Mama is in the hands of God now." She gently turned their faces from the scene, took their hands in hers and led the silent children down the street.

Marta, Anna, and the children had lived together in this part of the city since Anna's husband disappeared in the fighting. They spent each day waiting for him to contact them, but he never did. On her way home from her job at the university, Marta had been picking up some shopping when an elderly woman entered the market screaming that there had been another attack. Marta had already heard the missile whistling through the air. She never imagined it would be her home that crumbled into dust this time. She ran through the chaotic streets clutching her bag of groceries. As a treat, she had bought the special bread they all loved. The children called it Marta's bread.

Their house was reduced to a pile of rubble. Marta scrambled through the stones looking for their possessions, until the rescue men prevented her.

"You can't go in there," said a swarthy man, taking hold of her sleeve and pulling her away. "This building is about to collapse further. It's too dangerous."

She allowed herself to be led from the remnants of their home; all strength had ebbed away from her. She was directed to the communal shelter where at least they would be fed and given a change of clothes. Karim and Elena had still not uttered a word, and she could see in their huge dark eyes the shock of what had happened to them. Anna's body would be buried in a mass grave along with the other shattered bodies, some unrecognisable. On the day of the burial, Marta went to stand alongside the deep hole which would be the final resting place of her beloved sister. The stench from the grave was indescribable and she held her scarf across her mouth and nose. She prayed that Anna would find peace in the hereafter and threw a rose into the deep chasm where her body lay.

"Goodbye, Anna, may you find rest. I resolve to keep your children safe, no matter what it takes." With that she turned and made her way back to the building where the kind aid workers looked after the devastated human beings made homeless by this latest assault on their lives.

"This cannot continue to happen," she whispered. "There must be somewhere safer for us to live."

They had left the shelter the previous morning and made their way out of the city towards the blue hills in the distance. The aid workers had tried to persuade her to stay, but she refused. When they realised she was determined, they had supplied her with blankets and sleeping bags and a little food. She had no idea where they were going, but she knew they could not stay here in their shattered hometown. The war-torn countryside told its own tale with destroyed villages and dead and rotting livestock lying in the fields and by the side of the road. She had tried to avert the children's eyes from the horror, but they were curious. Death has a fascination for the young. Karim wanted to poke the skeletons with a stick blown from a splintered tree. Marta had told the children they were going on an adventure.

"Are we going to find Mama there?" asked Elena.

"No darling," Marta answered, her heart breaking, "but we will find a new house."

"Will Papa be there?" queried Karim.

"No, I don't think so, Karim, but we will make a home together where there are no bombs and we'll eat Marta's bread every day," she answered.

They seemed to be satisfied with this response for the

moment and skipped along the road. Marta admired their resilience and ability to accept their situation without real question. She knew there would be a price to pay further down the line, but for now they were content, if sad. She would never be able to be reconciled with what had happened.

They had walked for many hours up into the jagged hills which surrounded the town, resting only at midday in the shade of a rock until the afternoon cooled down. The children had slept, but she had been sitting there wide awake, alert for danger, trying to make plans. Just as the dusk was falling, they had come across the cave. The entrance was sheltered by sparse bushes. Marta parted the branches and crept into the darkness. It seemed safe enough; no one would be able to see them hiding there. Karim scrabbled in after her eager to be inside. He grinned at Marta. "Are we really going to sleep here?" he asked, already exploring the rocky interior of the cave.

Elena held back, clinging to Marta's skirt and hiding behind her legs. Her dark eyes darted around the cave before meeting Marta's. Marta gave her a reassuring hug and helped her over the loose stones at the entrance.

"I can pretend I'm a soldier hiding from the enemy," declared Karim, brandishing his stick, and slashing at the air. "I could make a campfire."

"No, you cannot," replied Marta. "You must be quiet and the light from the campfire would let people know we are here. This is our own special cave; we don't want anyone to join us, do we?"

"I suppose not," replied the disgruntled Karim.

"You must protect your sister, she's only little and is frightened. She's not as brave and grown-up as you," Marta said. "You can help me unwrap the blankets and sleeping bags and arrange where we are going to spend the night."

Feeling important, Karim set about unrolling the bedding and arranging it around the floor of the cave. He jumped when a bat flew overhead. Elena screamed. Marta cuddled the little girl and told her there was nothing to be afraid of; that the bat could not harm her. Marta spread their few rations on a cloth to keep them from the dirt and bat droppings and the children ate hungrily. Marta did not eat but sipped the bottle of now tepid water. They would have to find somewhere to source water tomorrow.

After she had settled the children in their sleeping bags, she sat at the cave entrance and watched darkness settle over the city. Sparse streetlights twinkled. She heard the missile screech overhead, fired from somewhere above and behind her, and watched as it burst in a flash of red over someone's dwelling. The rumble of another falling building filled the quiet of the night, and the anguished screams of dispossessed residents would haunt her for ever.

She lay down beside her nephew and niece, huddling with them to keep warm. Elena cried in her sleep, tears forming on her delicate face. Karim struck out with his arms, as if defending himself.

Marta didn't know how many hours they had been hiding in the cave, but the sun was rising. Streaks of red painted the horizon and a gentle breeze wafted along the opening in the hillside. The children were restless, twisting their blankets, flinging their arms around in their sleep. She felt water drip onto her headscarf; this cave was damp and musty, the walls glistening with moisture. Below, she could hear gun shot and shouting, see plumes of smoke and flame rising into the air from the bombs which had fallen on the town during the night. Now it was morning and she had to carry on. She would have to rouse the children soon, so they could continue their journey before the midday heat of the sun assailed them.

She woke the children and made them dress themselves. There was only a small amount of cheese and plain bread left, so she shared it out between them all. She gathered up their belongings and peered out of the cave. There was no one around that she could see, so she ushered them back to the rocky path they had been following the previous day. They walked until midday when the sun was too hot to continue and Elena tired. Karim put a brave face on it, but she could see that he was also struggling. Marta found a shady place in a hillside crevice where they could rest. She closed her own eyes, exhausted with the effort of climbing and staying alert. She was woken by a loud scream from Elena.

"Marta, Marta!" the girl shouted. "Look there. It's horrible. I'm scared."

Marta looked over to where the Elena was backed up against a striated stone.

"Keep still, Elena," she whispered. "Do not move whatever you do." A huge scorpion, black and evil looking, was scuttling in front of the child, its tail raised upright ready to strike. Karim had now woken and was staring at the creature. He picked up his stick, but Marta motioned at him to keep still.

"It will strike if you move, Karim, put the stick down slowly. Try to move closer to me without making any sharp movements." She held out her hand and the boy took it, shuffling sideways towards her. Marta could feel the sweat beads gathering on her forehead, trickling down her face and into the crevice between her breasts. Karim continued to stare at the creature. Marta saw that Elena was rigid with fright, her brown eyes wide open, and her face had a pallor which was frightening. She had to think of something to do.

"OK, Karim, give me your stick and my blanket. I'll try and distract the scorpion. Get ready to run over here,

Elena." Elena stared at her blankly. "Elena, concentrate, do as you're told."

Elena nodded, silent tears forming on her eyelashes and sliding down her cheeks.

Marta summoned all her courage and gripped the blanket; one false move and Elena would be fatally stung. As she moved closer the insect moved around in the direction of the shifting sound of the sand under her sandals; its feet scratching the soil. Its tail was erect over its head and Marta could see the swollen yellow tip full of poison. It was now or never.

"Run, Elena, run," she shouted as she flung the blanket as hard as she could.

Fortunately, it fell directly on the scorpion and she could see the creature rushing around in panic under the cloth, its tail jerking. She picked up Karim's stick and hit the frantic insect as hard as she could. It fell still, but Marta was not convinced it was dead, so she hit it again and again until a wet stain spread over the woollen fabric. She slumped down on the ground, weeping hysterically while the children looked on in horror.

"Marta, is it dead?" said Karim coming over to her, "Are you alright?" He put his arms around her neck, and she cried into his shoulder. She gathered herself together and began to stuff their belongings into a bag, avoiding her blanket.

"Come on, children, we must leave this place quickly. That creature might have relatives in the area," she said, trying to make light of the situation now it was over.

After a couple more days hiking and finding safe resting places each night, they had reached the top of the hill and were now walking down the other side, slipping, and sliding on the loose shale. In the distance, Marta could see some palm trees. Perhaps there was a village or an oasis, so she could fill the water bottle again and find some food. Or it might be a mirage, she couldn't tell.

"We'll rest for a while here, my darlings, in the shade of this rock. Do you see over there?" She pointed towards the trees. "There may be a village and if it is safe, we should be able to find food and water."

The children slumped against the tall stone and closed their eyes. Marta was dozing when she heard falling rubble and was instantly awake. There were voices coming towards them. They were male voices. What if they were soldiers? She hoped that whoever it was would not see them. They were partially hidden by the shady side of the stone which faced away from the road. Karim had also woken at the sound and was about to speak. Marta quickly covered his mouth with her hand and indicated to him to stay quiet. His eyes were wide, and above her hand, she could see her fear reflected in them. The clatter of boots was coming closer and a shower of pebbles fell on their heads. Marta gathered Elena close to her and raised her finger to her lips, begging the children to be silent. A tall shadow fell over them.

"What have we here?" the man's guttural voice echoed around the hills. He was tall and lithe and wore khaki trousers and a black shirt. On his head there was a beret identical to the ones worn by the soldiers they saw creeping around the streets of their town. There was another shower of pebbles and a second men joined the first.

"A woman and some children," the second soldier replied. "What shall we do with them?"

Karim wriggled from Marta's grasp; all fear gone.

"Leave us alone, we are doing no harm!" he shouted.

Marta held tightly onto Elena who was now whimpering. She didn't know what to do. She wanted to grab Karim and run, but that might be the wrong thing to do and would get them all killed. The soldier moved closer to Karim and prodded him in the chest.

"Brave little fellow aren't you, but foolish," he laughed. "And you, young lady, what are you doing out here with two children in tow?"

The man had kindly eyes, but Marta wasn't sure she could trust him.

"We were bombed out of our home, and we're going in search of a place to live. My sister was killed, and I vowed to keep her children safe." Marta gulped. She could feel tears coming but she didn't want this soldier to see. "It shouldn't be like this; we shouldn't have to live in fear all the time."

By this time, the rest of the men had caught up with the leader and they were all peering closely at Marta and the children.

"We could kill them and leave them for the vultures to eat," suggested the tattooed man with the ragged black beard.

"Or we could take them hostage and demand a ransom for them," said the man with crossed eyes. Elena cried out. Marta shushed her.

"Shut up all of you," said the leader. Turning to Marta, he said, "My name is David. These are my men. You will come to no harm with us." With that he scowled at the men and motioned for them to carry on down the hill. "Come, young man," he gestured to Karim, "let me help you gather up your things and I will escort you to the village where you can find shelter."

Unsure of what the man might do, Marta felt she had no option but to follow. Karim picked up their blankets, all the time watching the soldier with the blue eyes. Together they scrambled down the hill, Marta holding tightly to Elena's hand.

When they reached the edge of the village where the houses began, Marta saw that the town was whole. The palm trees she had seen were growing around a small lake and were heavy with fruit. The roads were busy; cars were hooting and donkeys braying. She heard women shouting at their children and dogs barking. She smelled the aroma of frying pastries and onions and the stench of donkey droppings. Clean washing was fluttering on lines strung across the roofs of the white painted houses. There were no bombed out buildings, no rubble lying in the street. She looked up at David.

"Where is this place?" she asked. "It is so peaceful. There is no war here."

"You have crossed over the hill into a new land. You will be safe here. I will take you to my mother and she will find you somewhere to stay. Follow me."

"But what about your men, the soldiers, I thought you were going to kill us. Is this a trap?" she asked, prepared to snatch the children and make a run for it. She knew she wouldn't get far, but at least she would have tried.

"You are safe with me," David said, picking up her bedrolls and bag. "My men are not soldiers; they are shepherds out looking for lost sheep in the hills. They should not have frightened you, I'm sorry for their behaviour.

Marta met David's blue eyes with her brown ones and nodded. Karim was standing by David's side, the child's eyes shone with trust. It was the first time since the bombing he had looked happy; she would count on his instinct. Marta took hold of Elena's hand as they walked across the square towards a large house on the corner. They were safe for now, but she wouldn't hesitate to move on if that safety was threatened. She was sure of that. She looked up at the bright blue sky and silently let her sister know that the children were safe.

"Will we have Marta's bread for tea?" enquired Elena, pulling at Marta's skirt as they crossed the dusty road.

About the author

'Yorkshire born, Liz has now moved from Anglesey to return home to North Yorkshire, where she spends her time writing short stories, poetry and completing her novel about her first love, Anglo-Saxons and Vikings. She is co-editor and contributor to *Reconsidering Gender, Time and Memory in Medieval Culture* (D. S. Brewer, 2015) and has been published in five Bridge House Anthologies: *Baubles, Glit-er-ary, Crackers, Nativity* and *Mulling it Over* and on *CaféLit Magazine* website. When inspiration dries up, she talks to her dog and gazes at her beautiful garden.

May's Resolution

Barbara Ratcliffe

You can leave Hong Kong but it will never leave you
Nuly Vittachi

Leicester Square was chaotic, filled with people, smells
wafting from the restaurants, red and gold lanterns hanging
from the shop fronts. It was a preview of what was to come.
The man at the travel agent seemed to understand. His kind
eyes, slightly shabby clothes and reassurances that it was a
safe place to go was all the encouragement that May needed.
As she snapped the clasp on her handbag shut with her ticket
safely inside she exhaled. This was the easy part. It was the
questions, that would come later that would be harder.

May wanted, no, needed to have this adventure but her
family were struggling to come to terms with it.
Understandable she supposed. They had a picture of her –
sensible, practical, self-effacing Mum. Always ready with
tea, freshly baked cakes and meals. Forever concerned
about their welfare: were they okay eating enough, sleeping
enough, earning enough? This need to travel halfway across
the world to reawaken memories of a previous life was a
mystery to them.

She hadn't talked about her early life in Hong Kong to
them. Her years in an internment camp, although forged
indelibly on her memory, were not something she wanted
to describe. And her life after that, an oasis of luxury with
the privilege that Jim's job had brought, was such a contrast
to her present life. It was easier to blot it out rather than
remember how life had been.

So many voices in her head – her children excited about

her big adventure, her interesting past. But there were definite undertones of worry. Should she be doing this alone – she'd never flown before? All her trips before had been by P&O liner, a long, luxurious way to travel.

She had taken her first flight in sixty years and survived the steep scary descent through high rise housing to land on a narrow runway in Kowloon Bay. Despite her aching muscles and a tiredness that had seeped into every part of her there was a spark of excitement that refused to be extinguished. Depositing her meagre luggage at the budget hotel, she changed into some cotton trousers and a loose blouse. Her room was sparse, just a single bed and chair, but she didn't want to waste her money on fancy rooms. There was so much more to spend it on here.

As May stepped out onto the street she was instantly drenched in sweat. She had forgotten how humid this city was.

The smell was the first thing that she noticed. Fishballs, noodles and beef, mixed with sweat and traffic fumes.

She craved to be part of this bustle again. although aware that at her age, and now unfamiliar with both its streets and rhythm, she may struggle. The contrast with the sleepy London suburb she had come from could not have been more marked. Every sense was on high alert – from the pungent smells to the chatter of people, so many people in a small congested space. Mothers laden with heavy bags and children. Old men smoking, spitting, laughing to reveal a few nicotine-stained teeth. Young teenagers jostling, parading their latest clothes and trying to find some space just to hangout and make their voices heard amongst the din.

She managed to find her way to the nearest tram stop and joined the throng boarding. With luck and determination, she squeezed into a narrow wooden seat by the open window of the tram. As the rickety double-decker made its way along

Kennedy Road she breathed a sigh of relief. After what had felt like a lifetime trapped in the sleepy London suburbs where she didn't fit in, she was finally back in Hong Kong. She felt alive.

It didn't take long for the jet lag to kick in. She needed to go back to her hotel and get some rest.

The next morning she woke to the familiar smell of Hong Kong – the mix of sweat and cooking.

She went downstairs and into the soupy morning fug to the congee shop on the corner. She ordered a steaming bowl of boiled rice with pork, and the surly waitress sloppily put it down, spilling some onto the greasy table. Hong Kong service, May smiled, savouring the texture and aroma of the food.

Outside, the city throbbed. The clamour of voices, the bikes wobbling down the side streets, festooned with poles carrying baskets, carrying goods. The stream of taxis and bikes on the main roads competing with each other for space on roads that were too narrow. The rattle of trams in the background.

Had she really lived and loved in this city all those years ago?

A memory floated into her mind.

She was sitting with Jim in their apartment. Gleaming wooden floors, leather pouffes and mahogany cocktail cabinet. A life of bridge parties, silk dresses, cocktails – luxurious, exotic.

Yes, this had been part of her life here after the war but there were so many darker pieces of the puzzle to put together.

She left the congee shop with the taste of the salty meat and creamy rice on her lips.

The bus ride was a rollercoaster. Her old bones felt every jolt as the driver negotiated the bends of the hills.

"Stanley Prison," the driver called, signalling the end of the journey.

May hesitantly stepped off the bus and blinked in the sunshine. It was eerily quiet, but in her head different voices from the past demanded her attention.

The years rolled away and she was back in camp. The memory was overpowering.

The squalor, too many human bodies crammed into confined spaces. She stumbled through the grounds only half aware of where she was going. Her head ached from trying to process these images that kept coming. As she sat on the wooden bench overlooking the prison grounds, tears fell.

The humidity hung over her, enveloping May in a sticky embrace.

She walked on till she came to the small group of headstones. Christmas 1941, brave men trying to get messages out, paying with their lives.

The Japanese had been brutal warders and the execution of these men showed the worst of this. For the rest in camp it was the occasional slap for not showing respect, and the slow but steady deprivation of food, light, electricity and space.

As she turned away May felt a burden lift. It was as if she was turning a corner and was heading back to the land of the living.

Back in the heat of the city the hotel was a beacon of serenity and opulence surrounded by chaos, and she headed for the Mandarin.

This symbol of luxury had been her regular meeting

haunt as a young carefree working girl. Before the war and the Japanese soldiers changed May's life forever.

About that author
Having retired from full-time teaching and adjusting to semi-retirement Barbara has time to indulge her lifetime ambition to write. This is her first piece of fiction she has submitted and it's based on events in her mother's life.

Mr and Mrs Lander

Mark Kristen

Frank Lander had never liked mornings.

His wife, Jenny, a full-breasted little tweak of a thing always woke up with sunlight in her eyes. Even though the day outside might be balmy and grey, she always found something to smile about. Frank called her his morning cricket, forever chirping.

If he had a smidgen of her upbeat persona he knew he would feel better. But he didn't. He didn't have her either. The thought of another day alone made him queasy. It had been three months since she'd shared his bed; three long months since they had made love, and it was all his fault.

"Jesus, Jenny," Frank clawed at his greasy hair, "how the hell did we get here?"

Brimming with last night's liquor he threw back the musty bedsheets and staggered to the bathroom, where he dipped in his bag, pulled out a razor and checked the mirror. He looked like a homeless person; a street liver: all matted hair, dead eyed and spiritless, waiting for death.

Post shave, he turned his clean face left then right, and growled, "You *bastard*!" His model looks had gained him all his soul desired, and a lot of problems too. He detested being the image of his late father. "You are where my problems lie," he told his reflection. "You were no father to me, and no husband to Mum."

The negative influence that had saturated Frank's childhood resurfaced, bringing with it vivid memories of the many times he had witnessed the female 'friends' of his father arrive unannounced at the door, loud in voice with hands flailing, shouting at Frank's gentle, caring mother, telling her of all of the broken promises her husband had made them, and what a pig he was.

She didn't need telling, she knew all too well what her husband was about.

Usually she would just shake her head and get on with her chores, but this time, after closing the front door, she flopped onto the sofa. When she looked up, a single tear glistened as it ran down her cheek.

"Are you OK, Mum?" Frank knew she wasn't.

"He promised me he would never do it again but he'll never stop. I'm sorry, Franky, I know he's your father and I shouldn't say it but I can't trust a word he says, and it's killing me."

"Why don't you leave him?"

"It's not that easy." When Frank rushed over and hugged her, she ran her fingers through his hair, "Oh, you're such a lovely boy."

"I hate him, Mum. If I was big enough I'd beat him up."

"When you get married, Franky, promise me you'll look after your wife and be good to her."

"I promise."

She stood up and straightened her apron. "I'd better get the tea on, he'll be home soon."

Two years later; when Frank was barely fourteen, unable to take anymore, in a fit of depression his mum took her own life, leaving him shattered. All these years later, still cursing himself for not being able to save her, he punched the shower button, hurried in, reached for the loofah, and scrubbed until his arms ached. But no matter how hard he rubbed, he still he felt dirty.

A hospital bed was his father's only companion when his lifestyle finally caught up and left him riddled with the pox, as penniless as a tramp and with fewer friends than a child molester has in prison. According to the death report Frank's guardians received, he drew his last breath in the early hours. "Surrounded by darkness," Frank, by then seventeen, scoffed, "and whatever ghouls might have been waiting for him, to wreak their revenge on the misery he had caused in their lives."

Drying himself down, Frank hated to admit it but he was more like his father than he realised. He splashed on some aftershave, dressed quickly, dropped down the stairs and strolled into the kitchen with a false, cheery, "Morning, Jenny, did you sleep well?"

Focussed on an imaginary black spot, scrubbing the marble worktop hard enough to take the sheen off, Jenny snorted.

"I said morning, Jenny." The bright cupboards and gleaming sink told Frank she had been up all night again. When he saw her bloodshot eyes he felt as if he'd been kicked in the stomach. She reminded him of his mum.

"Why did you do it?" She sighed. "What did I do that was so wrong?"

"You did nothing wrong... I still love you, Jen."

"Oh yes of course you do, *Francis.*" When she found out about his affair, Frank went straight from darling, or love, or Frank, straight to Francis. And he'd been Francis ever since.

"I'll do anything," he said.

"You've done enough."

"I want to put things right, Jen. I just want to help."

"Tell me something." Jenny slapped the cloth down, glared at him. "How does fucking someone else help then? Tell me that." Her neck veins swelled, she grew with them, "*Well?*" They were like worms under her skin. "Don't look down there." Worms on the march. "Look me and *tell me how that is supposed to help!*" She clasped her forehead. "I might have been able to handle a stranger, but why Amy? Why sleep with my friend?"

"I don't know what to say."

"Well, I do." She pointed to the door.

"Move out?" Frank stood rooted. "Surely you don't mean that?"

"Believe me, I mean it!"

Frank had never noticed before, but one of the kitchen floorboards had a split down the middle. Oh how he wished that fissure would open up like a sinkhole and suck him in.

"I'm going to work." Jenny pushed past him.

"Jen, please—" He held her arm.

"Just fuck off, will you, Frank."

Frank's breath caught. She used the shortened version of his name. *Maybe...* he thought... *maybe she's ready to forgive me...* But when she shoved his hand away and stomped upstairs to get dressed, that breath left him in a rush.

The front door closed and in the devastating silence, Frank recalled how, long before he met Jenny, he had felt that something was missing. He was tired of having one-night stands, and found himself gazing at couples walking hand in hand in the park, chatting intimately, or lying on a blanket lapping up the sun, maybe having a picnic, stealing kisses. He didn't want to get drunk anymore and wake up next to a strange woman. He wanted to love someone, and be loved back. With his mates he laughed and joked in his usual way, but deep inside he was empty.

As the months ticked by, unable to find anyone he clicked with, Frank was on the cusp of giving up when, in his hurry to get to work one morning he ran straight out in front of Jenny's car and she knocked him over. Luckily, she was slowing up for the traffic lights. Frank wasn't injured, just little shaken.

Even before he was on his feet she was out of the car remonstrating with him. "Are you some kind of idiot?"

Used to women fawning over him, not putting him in his place, Frank was quite taken with her smart, office style of dress, thick, wavy blond hair and emerald green eyes. He clambered to his feet and stood towering over her. Giving her his best smile, with a wink he asked why she had tried to kill him. But his cheeky chappie persona wasn't working.

"Didn't your mother teach you how to cross the road?" Her hand came up in a stop sign. "Don't bother answering that. I have no interest in what you've got to say."

"Are you always so rude?" Frank asked, aghast. Happy to admit he had been stupid, he thought he might get scolded, but didn't expect the sort of over-reaction this person was handing out. Seeing her head drop and lip twitch, he softened his voice. "Are you OK?"

"You're right," she said, unable to look at him, "I am being *very* rude. I'm not normally like this, it's just that my father died yesterday and I'm still in shock."

Offering his condolences, Frank introduced himself and said his father had passed away too. "Do you mind if I ask your name?"

"Jenny," she said. "So, you've lost your father? You know how I feel then?"

Not wanting to start their relationship with a lie Frank admitted, "We didn't get on too well."

"But he was still your dad."

"Listen, Jenny, I don't feel right asking at a time like this, but if there's anything I can do, please will you take my number," he scribbled it on a piece of paper and handed it to her, "and let me know... I won't ask for yours, that's not what this is about. This really is just me saying I want to help if I can." As he walked away he looked back over his shoulder. "Sorry for running out in front of you and ruining your day."

"You haven't ruined my day," Jenny said. "You might have just made it."

"Right back at you."

Jenny did call; soon after she had laid her father to rest. "I wanted to say thank you."

"*Thank* you?" Frank was confused. "But *I* was the fool who ran out in front of *you*?"

"You were so nice to me"

"That's true," he agreed, then, in his cheeky way, asked, "I don't suppose you'll let me be even nicer to you and buy you dinner sometime? Like, tomorrow night?"

"How can I say no to an invitation like that?"

From the first date they were both smitten and within two years, were married and buying their own house.

If he had to give his days a colour, before Jenny, Frank would have said they were a dull copper. Ever since she came into his life, every second had been like polished gold.

Not long after they married they tried for a baby, and luck seemed to be on their side because within weeks Jenny's stomach began to swell, leaving the two delirious in their expectant state.

Two months on, Frank came home and found his wife lying on the sofa, sobbing. "*Jenny?*" he hurried over. "What's wrong, Babe?" He pulled her close. "What's happened?"

It took three tries before she could speak. "Everything was OK when I got up. I had a coffee, went for a shower and started washing my hair." Her hand slipped to her belly. "That was when my period came. It was heavy, Frank, so heavy." She clung to his lapel as if to keep herself afloat. The tears returned. "I knew I was losing the baby and... and

93

there was nothing I could do. I'm sorry, Frank, I'm so sorry."

"You have nothing to say—"

"I'm useless! I can't even carry a child."

"It happens sometimes, Jen," Frank said softly. "I don't know why, it just does." Growing up he had been taught that 'Real men don't cry'. He clenched his jaw and managed to keep control, but when Jenny buried her face in his shoulder, wailing, "That was our baby, Frank, our baby, our baby." For the first time since his mum's funeral, he allowed himself to weep.

That afternoon he had ordered a pram from Amazon. It was a Silvercross, the latest model. Light brown – Jenny's favourite colour – with big wheels, Frank thought it looked 'bouncy' enough to handle the bumps in the pavement, the kerbs on the roads and the dips in the paths. It was due to arrive in two days' time. A nice surprise for the mum-to-be.

He slipped onto the sofa, whispering, "It'll be OK, Jen. We'll get there in the end."

Wrapped in each other's arms, they comforted each other as best they could. The quiet of the evening; broken only by sniffles and coughs, went on forever, until sleep finally eased their pain.

The following day Frank cancelled the order for the pram.

Over the weeks a distance grew between them, and day by day that gap widened.

One morning things peaked. Exasperated, Frank said, "It wasn't my fault, Jenny, *so why blame me?*"

"I don't blame you," Jenny hollered. "I… Oh, I don't know. Just go to work will you."

"That's always your answer isn't it? Go to work. Go to work. Maybe I should go to work and not come back."

When Amy heard what was happening she called round to see Jenny. "It must be really hard on your husband," she said. "You know blokes. The only things they talk about is sports, beer or sex, and not always in that order."

"I suppose so."

"He must feel really lonely."

"If we talk," Jenny said, "it always ends up in a shouting match. I know it's unfair but I can hardly look at him these days... No, Amy, don't raise your eyes... yes... yes, I *know* it wasn't his fault, but I can't help it."

"Poor Frank," Amy said, looking sideways at her friend. "Maybe I'll talk to him."

With Frank being so open with his feelings Amy found it refreshing. "If only Rob would let me in," she said. "We've begun arguing a lot too, recently. I've suggested counselling but as you know, my other half is like a closed book." She stroked Frank's cheek. "I wish he was more like you. You are the sort of man a woman needs. I'm here for you."

Before long, convinced a divorce was looming, Frank fell into his old ways and things between him and Amy became physical. Regrets soon set in.

When he called an end to the affair Amy's demeanour changed. She stood with her arms crossed, staring at him. "Do you think you can just screw me and call it a day when you've had enough? What do you think I am, Frank, a whore?"

"I thought you understood."

"At first, yes, I did. But things are different now."

"How so?"

"I've fallen in love with you. I want us to be together."

When she couldn't get her own way she went home and revealed all to her husband.

Screeching to a halt, Rob and Amy arrived at the Landers'

door ready for a fight. Amidst the shouting Jenny pleaded, "Will someone please tell me what's going on?" A truce was called, which settled things long enough for her to make coffee, place it on the table and ask, "Now then, what is all this about?"

As they came her way she carefully plucked the words from the air, pieced together the cause of the madness and sat stunned to hear that Rob and Amy had an open marriage. According to Rob, "We agreed from the start to live and let live, but to keep it between us." When Jenny asked about loyalty he said, "Life is short, and being with one person isn't natural, not to us anyway."

"Then why so angry with *him*?" She flicked her head at Frank.

"Like I said, what Amy and I get up to should have been kept outside of any friendships. That was the deal."

"Amy?" Jenny said, her hands prayer-like, jammed between her knees.

The reply came in a casual, "Most people go their separate ways in the end so why save yourself for one?"

"It seems," Jenny pinched the bridge her nose; almost as if her ideas smelled bad, "that my way of marriage is old fashioned and boring. So *you*, Francis, you can do what you want. I'm finished with this relationship." With that, she took her leave and went to their bedroom until the visitors had left.

When Frank came up an hour later, bulging with excuses and apologies, Jenny flew at him. "*I don't need you.*" Her hand met his cheek. The slap could have been heard out in the street. "And to think I was going to have child with you. It's our anniversary this week. Thank you for such a lovely present, thank you very much."

As he wouldn't grant her wish and move out immediately, that evening while Jenny was in the garden on the phone to her mother, Frank was moving his belongings into the spare room. There was no wishing each other good night that night, only the spiking voice of Jenny telling him, "You have three weeks to move out before I put this in the hands of my solicitors."

Another morning arrived and Frank woke to the world he'd begun to hate. It had felt like a lifetime since the spare room had become his chamber, and he was only there thanks to the forgiving nature of his spouse, whose temper had long since depleted, though she still wanted him gone. He had spent most evenings lying on his bed in a drunken haze, staring at the ceiling searching for something to smile about.

Downstairs at the table Jenny nodded a curt hello.

Halfway through his breakfast toast, vomit filled Frank's throat. "You bitch," he bashed the table. "How could you do that to me?"

"*Don't* you bloody well dare, you hypocrite!" Jenny told him straight. "You were seeing Amy." She casually checked her fingernails. "Now I've been seeing Rob. What's the problem?" She reached for her nail file, as she did she looked up and smiled sweetly. "How do you like it, Francis... a taste of your own as they say?" When she added nonchalantly, "By the way, I thought you might like to know I'm pregnant." He nearly fell off his seat.

Frank composed himself enough to stand up and grunt, "I'm going to work."

The bang of the front door shook a few bricks loose.

Down on the tube platform jostling for space, when the first train rumbled in and the doors creaked open, a blast of heat hit Frank. Seeing the train packed tighter than a coffee shop in Amsterdam, he was not about to step into an airless tin cylinder, but he didn't have a choice. *Schindler's List* came to mind as the crowd surged forward and shoved him into the carriage. He fought a way back towards the platform, apologising to the mouths throwing obscenities his way for causing an obstruction, and squeezed himself out just as the doors closed.

By the time the next train rolled in, having calmed himself, Frank hopped aboard and stood by the door.

When the train left Kennington, a tad of envy tugged when he saw a traveller further up the carriage. Wearing a loose cotton jacket and baggy trousers, with his long hair and straggly traveller's beard, the guy looked as if he'd been up all-night partying. Thin lines around his dark eyes gave the impression he laughed a lot.

The train lurched into The Elephant and Castle where dozens of commuters fought their way on, forcing Frank up the aisle. Finding himself next to the traveller, he blurted, "Morning." He felt uncomfortable breaking the 'tube rules' which were: keep your head down, block your ears and ignore everyone else, but today he needed a distraction. The traveller stared straight ahead, he knew the tube rules. In the tightly-packed leather bag hanging over the guy's shoulder, Frank saw the outline of what looked like a beach towel, some spare clothing, maybe a snorkel and mask. "Going anywhere nice?" he said. "Somewhere warm, maybe?"

"Maybe?" The guy smirked, as if to say, "You're trapped in your little world whereas mine is wherever I want it to be."

"You haven't got room for me in there, have you?" Frank pointed to the bag and joked, "I need to get away too. Can I come with you?"

"You wouldn't fit in," the traveller said as a smartly-dressed woman in a blue trouser suit, wearing a lemony perfume, squeezed by him. He seemed to sneer at her, then leaned back, looked Frank up and down and half-smiled. "No, you would not fit in."

That comment stung Frank. He thought he was pretty sociable, and got on with most people.

"Where are you going, where wouldn't I fit in?" He asked, trying to hide the hurt in his voice.

"Paradise."

"And where is that exactly?"

"Guess. I'll give you three chances, and if you get it right, I'll take you in here." He patted his bag.

The traveller had an accent that Frank couldn't place; not that that mattered, this guessing game was keeping his mind off of his problems. "The Seychelles?" he said, and received a head-shake. "Thailand?" Another shake. "How about Sri Lanka?"

"No."

This guy had confidence. He didn't have to worry about bills, mortgages and the like, he was too busy travelling the world. Frank wanted some of that.

As the train charged along, the carriage lights flashed off and back on. The traveller's eyes widened, darted left and right. He looked furtively up and down the carriage, then back at his reflection in the darkened carriage window.

Frank understood the guy's claustrophobia. Just a train earlier he had experienced it himself for the first time ever. Struggling to keep Jenny out of his mind, he kept talking. "Being in a beautiful place certainly beats being here?"

"I agree," the traveller said. His calloused hand circled the air, his face became ugly and twisted. "This place is filth."

"Easy," Frank said, taken aback. "Everyone has to make living you know."

"All these people care about is money."

The guy seemed overly aggressive. *Life gets to everyone*

sometimes, Frank thought, *even relaxed dudes like this.* Then it occurred to him. "You're going to Goa, aren't you? To a yoga retreat to chill out?"

"You have had your three guesses."

Frank went to speak again but seeing the traveller staring straight ahead, having re-aligned himself with the tube rules, decided not to.

As the train slowed for London Bridge (Frank's stop) he decided to man-up. If his marriage didn't work out he would pack a bag and go off in search of a bit of paradise himself. The train pulled in, he wished the guy well. "Take care, mate."

"Have a nice life," the traveller said with a blank expression.

Amidst a long line of commuters shuffling along the platform; shoulder to shoulder like a waddle of penguins, Frank smiled to himself. They had only spoken briefly but he felt a connection with the traveller, and hoped one day they would meet again, maybe on the beach of some distant shore or somewhere – ***BOOOOMM!***

A deafening explosion shook the station. Frank's ears popped as a thick plume of smoke blew back from the tunnel and engulfed the commuters nearest to it. The electricity failed, people stumbled into each other in the dark. In seconds, London Bridge had switched from a busy transport hub to Lucifer's den. Gasping as the oily air circled them, people panicked and broke into a charge; running into the others further up the platform; Frank being one. Landing face first, the thought of never seeing Jenny again gave him the strength to heave the mountain of flesh off his back, battle to his feet and search for an escape route.

A little way up the platform, twinkling in the gloom like an orange star of Bethlehem, he spotted a sign: **WAY OUT** and headed for it. Just past the sign, an old woman was leaning against the wall with her hand on her chest struggling to breathe. People were shoving her to one side in their panic to get out. Seeing her about to collapse, Frank clutched her wrist and dragged her along beside him. When her legs gave way he scooped her up, shielded her from the smoke as best he could and fought a way up the escalators. Carefully holding his fragile package tight to his chest like a new born, he dipped his head and reassured her, "I've got you."

Eventually they fell into the street, spluttering into the arms of the rescuers where a white uniform took the woman and headed off. "Wait," Frank heard the lady say in a croaky voice. Her crooked finger pointed over the medic's shoulder towards him.

"Hey," the medic called out, "someone wants to speak to you."

Swiping the sweat from his face, Frank looked over.

"Thank you, young man," the old lady wheezed and coughed into her gnarled hand. "You saved my life. Your mother would be proud of you, and your wife is a very lucky woman."

The medic nodded before saying, "Come on, let's get you to hospital."

The last thing Frank saw of the woman, she was being stretchered into an ambulance. He wondered how she knew he was married, then realised he was caressing his wedding ring. Drained, he turned, slid down the wall and sat with his head between his knees, retching. A bottle of water appeared. Frank sunk it in one go. "Stay still, we'll be taking you next." The voice was calm and controlled, as were the hands that clamped a mask over his face. "Just relax and breathe as normally as you can." Air that smelt of incense blew lightly into Frank's face.

There were shadowy people now, bending down in

front of and standing to one side of him. They were all speaking but he couldn't make out what they were saying. Then his world closed in.

He felt like a baby wrapped in a blanket and held in a loving embrace. Everything was hazy, peaceful and calm. The emotional thunder that had been tearing him apart for months had faded. He wasn't Frank anymore, waking to a stomach full of knots, a weight on his shoulders and a thumping behind his eyes. Now, he was a solitary raindrop, clean and fresh, falling gently from a single, fluffy cloud. Above him, the blue sky spread out and filled his vision as he drifted downwards. A thought came, *I've been such an idiot.* He knew in that moment, if he wanted Jenny to forgive him, he had to reciprocate. *If I can do that, then maybe... just maybe...* a pressure came on his chest, a vicious jolt rocked him. Strangely, Frank felt no pain. A muffled voice said, "He's back!"

After he had been checked over and transferred onto a ward, a nurse told Frank, "We've called your wife and she'll be here soon. The main thing is that you're safe now, so try to get some rest."

When he woke up he was circled by machines that beeped constantly. Jenny cupped his hands. "I thought I'd lost you. I... I'm sorry, Frank, I know I can be really pushy and it was part my fault—"

"Amy was the biggest mistake ever, Jen. Please, can you forgive me? I can't live without you, I really can't."

Before she could reply, a TV newsflash caught their attention. It confirmed the explosion had been a suicide attack, carried out by an Afghan man of twenty-seven who the security services had been tracking, but they had lost him a week earlier. When a photograph of the bomber came up Frank gasped. It was the traveller.

"What's wrong?" Jenny asked.

102

Frank raised his hand as if to say, 'Don't worry.' He recalled pointing to the bag the traveller's bag, *"You haven't got room for me in there, have you? Can I come with you?"*

"You wouldn't fit in."

"Where are you going, where wouldn't I fit in?"

"Paradise... The word jerked in Frank's mind... *Paradise... Paradise!"*

"Frank?" Jenny's voice was on the rise. "Shall I call the nurse?"

"No, Jen, I'm OK... Really, I'm fine." He didn't have time to dwell on what happened. There was nothing he could have done to change it, but there was something he could do to change the future. "Jenny listen, I know it's not mine but I promise you this, I'll still love and care for the baby, and I'll do my best to be a good dad. I swear I won't let you down again. We can make this work if we really try."

Jenny raised her head and brushed her hair out of her emerald eyes. She looked distant.

"I was stupid," Frank said, "so damn stupid." He knew he was too late, and babbled on about it all being his fault, how he didn't blame her for not wanting to try, how sorry he was for messing it all up and how – he fell silent when Jenny placed her finger on his lips to quieten him.

She tipped her head to one side and smiled. "The baby's yours, Frank... I didn't sleep with Rob."

"Really?"

"I was being childish and stupid, and only said that to get back at you. I'm surprised you haven't noticed this." She leaned back and showed him her swollen belly. "I was going to tell you the day Rob and Amy came round that I was a month late. It was our anniversary that week and it would have been the best present I could have given you."

"I'm so sorry for spoiling that day."

Jenny shrugged. "We all make mistakes. I suggest we forget the past three months, and start over. What do you think?"

"I love you so much, you know that," Frank said with a cheeky grin, "even though you tried to kill me."

"*What?*" Jenny was flummoxed, then giggled when she remembered the day they met, when he ran out in front of her car.

"Meeting you is the best thing that's ever happened to me, Jenny."

"Right back at you." Jenny used the same words as Frank had when he was walking away that day.

A fresh start was calling, a new beginning, a new life. The most important person in Frank's, was here now, she still loved him, she was carrying his baby, and it wouldn't be long before she'd be taking him home.

About the author

Originally from Folkestone in Kent, Mark first began writing twenty years ago, on a whim. He was bored with life and fancied a challenge. Being a maintenance engineer, whenever work was quiet and he had nothing to do, to pass the time he decided to write a book. He took two wooden pallets up into the roof space of the factory he was working in, balanced a desk and chair on the pallets, ran an extension lead up, plugged a light in and spent the next year scribbling away while looking down through the tiles to where the factory workers were running around like a nest of ants. He never did get caught and decided to call the novel *Zach*. It tells the story of a young lad desperate to escape his boring existence by hitchhiking across Europe heading for a kibbutz in Israel. By the time he had finished writing that story Mark was hooked; he had caught the 'writing bug' and since that first novel has written a second novel, and lots of short stories.

Next Time, Maybe

Allison Symes

Wexton is a lovely place, honest.

It is a charming market town. Its War Memorial and its library are listed and I love the place.

Wexton is on the edge of a National Park and the only time the peace is disturbed is when some foolish cat tries to walk through the park when all of the dogs around here (and there are *loads*) go potty. They all do. It is a sight to see *and* hear, mind you!

Some people put bets on how long it will take the cat to get out of the park but I don't see how anyone can measure it. I've seen those cats go and boy, are they fast. It's strange how they never make the same mistake twice.

But the downside is everyone knows everyone else's business, especially mine.

I am known as the Resolute Queen.

The locals have a talent for sarcasm. It's a pity there are no marketing opportunities for it.

It's just I've broken more resolutions than I've eaten hot dinners, according to the locals. It's nonsense. I just know when something is not working out and I may as well stop beating myself up over it. It's obviously time to draw a line and move on. So I do. What's wrong with that? Life's too short to waste time on regrets.

The locals say I give up too soon. I have no staying power. Ha! What would they know?

Excuse me. I must just finish this delicious cream cake. We have a wonderful bakery called *Pam's Pastry Perfection* and if ever there was a place that lived up to its name, this is it. I want to just finish this cake because I know my *Slimming World* consultant often walks here at about this time dropping off her latest leaflets.

Naturally I don't want to be caught out. Well, not for the fifth time. I laughed it off the first three times, as did she. Her laugh sounded hollow the fourth time to be honest. I'd rather not hear it again.

Still at least she didn't catch me and my friend, Sharon, finishing a big tin of *Quality Street* between us in one sitting, the day after we both swore to diet. We didn't know we'd both sworn to diet. Honest. It was just I hadn't seen Sharon for years, not since our school days, and it was wonderful to have my best mate move back into Wexton. We had to celebrate, didn't we?

Okay, finishing a tin of *Celebrations* might have been more apt, but the *Quality Street* was all that we had to hand. It is also handy having a pal who adores the toffees!

Ah that's better, the cake was every bit as wonderful as it looked, but I must say I am sorry. Oh not for scoffing the cake but I didn't introduce myself properly, did I? My pals say I rush headlong into the latest new thing or race ahead with the conversation before anyone else gets a chance to join in and here I go *again*.

Well, anyway hello there. I am Sandra Holmes, happy spinster of this parish. I'm a blue-eyed, bespectacled, brunette midget and I work as a secretary for Clang and Sons, Estate Agents, on the corner of Cross Street and High Way.

Yes, I know. Someone has to work for them. And I do. They are all right but what hope do I have of sticking to a diet when everybody takes it in turns during the week to bring in the latest delicious confections from the delightful *Pam's Pastry Perfection?*

My brother, Tom, says it's to make up for the misery of being a heartless, money-grabbing estate agent, but he always has been cynical and his politics are to the left of Lenin, so he was never going to judge an estate agent fairly, was he?

106

Oh and Tom always accepts when *I* buy *him* a pie or sausage roll from *Pam's*. I am pleased about that, funnily enough. I'd have thought he was sickening for something if he ever turned anything down from there.

Anyway I thought I'd record my attempts at improving my life and it was good of you to turn up and read my tale. I thought I'd leave it here in this exercise book for you to find, right here on the old bench, and if I thought one person might be less judgmental on those folk who have trouble keeping resolutions, then writing my story would be well worth the effort. This writing business is hard work. I've never written anything as long as this before. But I do feel better for getting this out of my system.

I am fed up with being laughed at for my foibles. I don't pretend to be perfect. Other people break their resolutions, don't they? I can't be the only one. So why just pick on me?

Ah, there comes my *Slimming World* consultant. Fortunately, I'm not going to be weighed until next Monday so that gives me five days to burn that cake off. I should manage that.

I give her a cheery wave. Bless her, she smiles back. I think it's the polite, professional smile she uses. Hmm… Maybe she did see me eat the cake. I thought I was far enough round the corner to be out of sight. Oh well. I'll know when I weigh-in. She will say something if she did see me. She's probably contractually obliged to do so.

Mind, I must also remember to make sure my walks don't take me past *The Dog and Duck, The Wexton Arms,* or *The Green Man.* Those three places remind me of one of my more public 'failures'.

I'd decided to give up drink for a month. It was sheer bad luck on day four, (when the craving for a salted caramel *Baileys* was beginning to kick in, as it will), old Gavin calls out to me as I walk by. Well, I had to go and chat to him and see how he and his lovely wife, Ruthie, were doing. They're 160 between them if they're a day and it would've been plain rude of me not to stop by and have a chat. We had a lovely time.

Yes, I know. I should have stuck to the non-alcoholic drinks. I love a *J2O* as much as the next woman but Gavin and Ruthie were having *Baileys* themselves (she likes the chocolate one – she is a lady of excellent taste) so I thought I'd join them. Well, it was a social occasion and it did all three of us the power of good to put the world to rights over a glass or two of our favourite Irish drink.

I was laughed at for that. Several of my colleagues spotted me without me realising. I guess I should've known something of the sort would happen.

The only thing I learned from that debacle is to never tell the people you work with about your latest plan to 'self-improve'. They won't let you forget it if you get it wrong. They still haven't.

The only plus side is I get at least two bottles of *Baileys* as presents every Christmas. They laugh. I put on my best wry smile and then drink the lot over the holidays. It is the only thing to do I tell myself. Naturally I don't tell my *Slimming World* consultant and blame the Christmas cake (I don't eat it, funnily enough) or the *Quality Street* (and I've established my credentials there).

One thing I would love to know is why people think I'm weak-willed. If you're going to make a resolution, you've got to start as you mean to go on *and* then go on. That is the whole point, isn't it?

If it goes wrong, you're not going to get that back, are you? You may as well move on. My *Slimming World* consultant tells me I haven't got the idea. I did tell her I haven't given up on losing weight and becoming fitter, it's just I've accepted it will take me longer than I thought. *That* is okay. Even she said so.

I suppose consistency would be nice. And I don't mean consistently being the butt of other people's lame gags. What goes in to *The Wexton Arms* and wobbles? Answer: Sandra Holmes. Me! How hurtful is that? I do sometimes go in there and have one drink. Even I don't wobble after one drink – one bottle maybe but never one drink. Nobody sees that, do they? Where do they all suddenly disappear to then, that's what I want to know!

My most recent resolution was to increase my exercise. I've never been sporty so a good walk is how I keep fit. Was it my fault we had torrential rain, hail, snow, thunder and lightning, gales and the like all at the time I was going to start my new regime?

By the time the weather cleared, I'd lost interest. Walking does seem to be what old people do and I'm only twenty-eight. But the thought of a gym or swimming horrifies me and what with the sports places opening, then closing again due to You Know What, I suppose I am better off just walking. I wish it could be more interesting though.

I don't want to walk past *Pam's Pastry Perfection* more often than I can help. I'm trying to limit that to twice a week. Today is my second visit this week and it's only Tuesday!

But if I go the other major route around our town, I walk past the pubs. So what is a girl to do? I make life complicated for myself.

If only I could stop making resolutions…

Hmm… There's a thought.

My final resolution could be to stop making the dratted things. Nobody could laugh at me for that, could they? This is one I could keep! It could be fun to see the looks on everyone's faces when I tell them I'm quitting the resolution game. It would serve them right if they're disappointed, but tough. Into every life a little rain must fall and it would make a change for it not to fall on me.

Worth a go then! See you around and thanks for reading my story. I'm off for my walk, free at last. No more resolutions. No more let-downs! I will go where I want.

Just maybe I will decide I don't need that drink or wonderful cake. Hmm... Maybe that's going a bit far but perhaps if I don't feel the pressure of keeping a resolution going, I won't feel the need to have something to cheer me up when I fail. That must be worth trying.

This is it then. You have just met the new Sandra Holmes. Wish me luck!

About the author

Allison Symes, who loves reading and writing quirky fiction, is published by Chapeltown Books, CaféLit, and Bridge House Publishing. Her flash fiction collections, *Tripping the Flash Fantastic* and *From Light to Dark and Back Again* are out in Kindle and paperback. She has been a winner of the Waterloo Arts Festival writing competition three years in a row where the brief was to write to a set theme to a 1000 words maximum.

Her YouTube channel, with book trailers and story videos, is at www.youtube.com/channel/UCPCiePD4p_vWp4bz2d8oSJA/

With her non-fiction hat on, Allison blogs for online magazine, *Chandler's Ford Today*, often on topics of interest to writers. Her weekly column can be found at http://chandlersfordtoday.co.uk/author/allison-symes/

Allison also writes for *Authors Electric*, *Mom's Favorite Reads*, and *More Than Writers*, the blog spot for the *Association of Christian Writers*.

Old Flowers

Holly Jane

"What do we want for dinner?" She taps her head thoughtfully and clicks her tongue. I sit over on the cushioned windowsill opposite the family cat, Nero, who stares at me intently.

"Pie and mash perhaps?" I muse. She decides for a few more seconds and nods. She brings out a frozen pie and sets to work on boiling a bag of week-old potatoes. She doesn't seem to mind and hums tunelessly as she works, peeling the skins and cutting away the shoots.

"The garden's a mess," I call out as I stare lazily through the window. The cat follows my gaze. Predictably, she doesn't reply. I smile. She was never a green fingered goddess. It was her mother that I bonded with, over a mutual love of growing flowers and vegetables.

Sarah plates up the steaming dish and trots across the kitchen towards me. I move my legs and she curls up on the opposite side of the window seat, dinner perched precariously on her knees. It wobbles dangerously and makes me squirm, but she makes it work. Sarah was always good like that.

"What are you staring at, Nero?" She murmurs fondly and rubs him lightly behind the ears.

The next morning, she flits around the house in a mad rush as she tries to locate her belongings for work.

"Keys!" I bellow down the hall. A few moments later, she sighs and stomps back through the front door. She grabs the car keys from the side table and heads back out.

I shove my hands in my pockets and head down to the village myself. I wave to my neighbours as they start their

111

own car in the chilly autumn air. Mr Barnes grumbles as his old cat catches sight of me and trips him up in her hurry to get back into the house.

Despite the overcast skies, the air is crisp and fresh. I stretch and amble down past the promenade and in the direction of the pier. Towards lunchtime, I think about popping into the high street bakery to smell Sarah's freshly baked bread.

As usual, the woman is hard at work as she glides across the counter and delicately packages the baked goods her customers clamber for. The bakery is heaving with the lunchtime crowd, so I slip towards the back of the store and flash her an encouraging thumbs up every time she glances my way. I take my usual table in the corner by the window and scan the front pages of the newspapers on the rack. As the commuters slowly begin to filter out, she breathes a sigh of relief and wipes her face on her flowery apron.

As she's about to come and sit at my table for her break, the bell above the door tinkles softly and another customer walks in. He looks either late twenties or early thirties and good looking in a classical sort of way. He's dressed in a suit with a light waterproof jacket over the top. His brow furrows as he stares up at the menu above the counter.

"Can I help?" Sarah asks lightly as she brings a new tray of raspberry croissants out to the front. As she turns past the corner towards him, she catches herself on a cupboard handle and knocks the tray onto the floor, cursing under her breath.

"Sorry," he says, hands outstretched. "I didn't mean to interrupt you."

"You didn't really," she waves him away. "I'm just notoriously clumsy."

"No really, let me pay for them since they're unusable now. How much do I owe you?" Without waiting for a reply, he brings out a smart leather wallet. Even from the corner table, I can see it's filled with several cards. Sarah wisely decides not to argue further and steps gingerly over the ruined pastries towards the till.

"That's... A baker's dozen at £2.50 each. £32.50 altogether..." She says shyly. "You know what? Honestly, keep your money. It doesn't matter; it's my fault."

He smiles and hands over two crisp twenty-pound notes. "I won't hear any more about it. Please just take the money. I haven't even decided what I want to eat yet!" He laughs and makes a face. She beams back. An effortless gesture that makes my stomach turn.

"Why don't you take a seat? How about a coffee and a BLT on the house?" She hands him back his change and for the briefest of seconds, their hands are touching. My gut twists again, but it's nausea this time and I'm forced to continue to watch.

As he drags his laptop out of his bag and selects a table in the opposite corner, Sarah's eyes briefly flicker over to my direction. The table where we'd had out first impromptu date. She blinks and quickly moves on.

"How are you doing, Nick?" A man in an old grey suit greets me as I exit the bakery and head for the high street. I turn quickly to see if he's addressing anyone else by the same name.

"Do I know you?" I ask hesitantly.

He shakes his head and removes the matching bowler hat. "We've never met face to face before. I just wanted to check in with you, Nick. Make sure you're doing OK." He smiles encouragingly. His round face shines in the light of the afternoon.

"Just dandy," I say. My nerves are frayed with thoughts rolling around my head.

"A lot of sadness there," the old man says. "I bet you're feeling quite alone."

"Aren't we all *alone*, in some way?" I snap. The man doesn't seem to mind my snippiness and invites himself to stroll along the road with me. His walk briefly reminds me of my own grandfather and there's another lump in my throat I can't seem to clear.

"You don't have to be alone, Nick," he says. "But there are some things you'll need to let go of first." He glances pointedly back down the street towards the Daisy Chain Bakery. I'd helped her paint it a handsome shade of light blue while she used her A-level art skills to paint intricate wildflowers around the windows and door. We'd saved together and worked crappy jobs for five years to make her dream come true.

"I can't," I swallow eventually. "Please – just stop following me. Leave me alone."

"Have a good day, honey," I murmur as Sarah yawns and slips out of bed next to me to go downstairs for her morning orange juice. Try as I might, I struggle for sleep and I toss and turn. The butterflies are back in my stomach, but now they feel like bats with huge leathery wings. The kindly old man's face is in my head again, cocky and so sure of himself, I think. He didn't know me from Adam.

It's Saturday morning, which means Sarah usually only works half the day until the weekend girls take over from lunchtime. I don't bother to walk down the village again today, so I roam round the garden and make mental notes of the things that need to be done before the summer arrives. The sunlight spills through the French doors and

114

fills the house with the smell of pollen and next door's barbeque.

The sounds of shoes scuffing against the entry hall carpet brings me back inside and I grin, ready to welcome her home. When Sarah enters, my grin slips and she's dragging in from the bakery the businessman she'd met the day before.

"Thanks," he says as Sarah hands him the cordless home phone. "I have coverage, so they're usually here within the hour." He smiles sheepishly and presses the mobile phone from his pocket again. The screen is smashed.

"The car's in a pretty safe neighbourhood." She shrugs. "Your phone, I can't help with. You are welcome to stay for a coffee though while you wait? Or tea?"

"Whatever's the least amount of trouble for you," he replies and sighs at the sight of the phone. "I'll have to figure out how to get my files off this thing, when I get back. I'll call the provider later and get the insurance on it."

"Right, you're a couple of towns over?"

He nods and she pulls out a seat at the breakfast table, which he takes. "Yes. Business takes me around the region, but that's where I am mostly. How about you? You been a village girl all your life?"

She giggles and turns to fill up the kettle as he dials from the home phone. He doesn't notice, but I see the pink blush crawl up from her shoulders and into her hair.

"Are we going to be OK, Sare?" I murmur quietly.

Sarah starts to spend just that little bit longer in the mirror, when she gets up for work. It starts small, just a splash of foundation here and there. Eyeshadow, eyeliner, lip gloss. She transforms before my very eyes and I'm too scared to look at her before she leaves in the mornings.

"Have a good day, sweetheart." I say quietly as the door

115

slams. I decide to spend the day at the pier and spend hours trawling up and down, staring at the amusements and food carts. I'd been staying away from the high street and the bakery for the past few weeks. Sarah doesn't seem to notice. She chats enthusiastically with the suited man almost every day as he passes through for lunch. I come to learn that his name is Regan. The name sounds special when it tumbles out of her mouth and he gives he that smile that makes my stomach hurt.

I'm at the end of the pier and my legs dangle over the side. I'm gazing into the sea below that I don't even register there's someone sitting next to me, until he coughs politely.

"You again," I say rudely as soon as I see that round face. He says nothing, but neatly arranges his pressed trousers and skips popcorn into the sea along with me. Neither of us start a conversation, but it was different to have some real company for a change. I think of Sarah and long to go home and hold her for hours.

"Who are you?" I sigh. The lights from the ships in the distance begin to glare out over the darkening sea. Around us, the amusements are being switched off and the smells of food are long gone. Even in the overhead lamp lights, his face still has a weird sheen to it.

"A friend," he replies gently. "No one you need to worry about, son." He chuckles good-naturedly and again, the friendly grandfather feeling returns. There's even an old pipe in his breast pocket of his waistcoat. I feel my anger and frustration deflate as I stare into the cold depths below.

"I don't think I can keep up with this guy," I say between gritted teeth. "He muscles into my house, my life and my girl. Fabulous Mr. Perfect with his shiny Mercedes and bags of money dangling out of his ass."

116

"I don't think there's anything we can do," my companion says quietly, but he looks sympathetic. "That's the beauty of letting go, son."

"I'm not going to let her be taken by Mr. Oxford University." I snap.

"It's not your decision," is the calm reply and the bowler hat comes off again as he rolls it from one hand to the other. I say nothing more but continue to stare into the inky sea and think about how wrong he is.

Mr. Knight in shining armour keeps visiting the house, despite my loud and violent outbursts over Sarah's shoulder when she answers the door to him, but she continues to welcome him into our home, all smiles and fruity smelling perfume. More than once, I interrupt the longing glances between them and kick the wall in the next room.

I realise that through jealousy and anger, I can manipulate the world around me and leave my mark. I test this out the first night Regan is invited to spend the night at the house. As soon as the bedroom door slams shut behind them, I kick it back open and watch as they scramble worriedly apart from one another.

When he's asleep, I lean over him and gently flick his temples, so he awakens in a panic and rubs his head in confusion. I patiently take an old wicker seat on the other side of the room and wait for him to go back into deep sleep, so I can do it all over again.

"When did he pass away?" Regan says a couple of days later over breakfast. I smile to myself at the way he yawns into his fried eggs. Sarah takes a moment to swallow and drop her gaze.

"Last year," she says finally. "But it feels like he's here sometimes. Still pretty fresh, you know?"

"Sounds rough," he says with a soothing voice that makes me want to vomit. She barely registers that he's spoken, already looking off down the garden. I don't need to see what she's looking at, to know it's the old flowers we planted together.

"I was so *angry* when he died," she says quietly. "How dare he be my rock for so many years and just disappear into nothingness like that? I kept walking around the house for hours, expecting him to be there but he wasn't. Took me a long time to forgive him."

"And do you now?" Regan says.

She takes a minute to think and nods slowly. "Yes, I do. I really hope he's at peace, enjoying himself. Taking a rest."

I turn to her slowly and my heart lurches with guilt. I realise it's the first time since I died, that she truly looks at peace with herself too. She's still staring at those damn flowers, but there's a small hint of a smile and I knew that she was letting me go.

I feel him appear before I turn around; the gentleman in the bowler hat is there. He's waiting for me to speak first. As if worried she would overhear, I move outside of the front door and try to breathe deeply.

"Who will protect her and look out for her?" I say mournfully. My voice cracks, but I'm too emotionally drained and exhausted to be embarrassed in front of him.

"You've done your bit, and you've done a great job with her. Look how healthy she looks now, how happy."

"You think she'll forget me?"

"Not a love like that," he says gently and opens the back door of a taxi that's waiting in front of the house. I take a few more minutes to gaze up at the old Victorian brickwork, the rickety roof tiles, the neatly painted windows and the sounds of Sarah laughing airily within.

And then I get into the taxi.

About the author

Holly Jane an aspiring writer by night, training Veterinary Nurse by day. Aside from tending to a house of animals that include twelve house rabbits, two cats and a long haired Chihuahua with the grace of a Great Dane, she can usually be found hunched over her desk with a lukewarm forgotten tea in hand and a computer full of projects. She is currently working on her first novel *Beneath the Door*, which she's hoping to release late 2021. Occasionally she likes to dabble in short stories and has an unhealthy obsession with cheesy chips.

Pandora's Basket

S. Nadja Zajdman

In spring, Montreal's Goyer Street teemed with kids. They
bounced their rubber balls against buildings and raced their
bikes to the schoolyard; they played stick hockey in the
street, stick-handling around the moving vehicles of irate
drivers. Their mothers sat vigil on the balconies of three-
storey flats. From their perches the women exchanged the
latest recipes, the latest gossip, and shouted at their kids to
keep them from landing under cars.

All, except Nehama's mother. When she wasn't helping
her husband in the store, she was holed up in her bedroom,
reading. She never shouted from the balcony – she never
allowed Nehama to, neither.

Nehama's mother kept away from the neighbourhood
women and from the primitive, pulsing life of the street.
She wore scarves to cover the scar at her throat and cowered
at the sound of airplanes. She kept her door locked.

These days, Nehama's mother remained more aloof
than ever. She stayed inside for hours, poring over the
photographs she kept in a yellow sewing basket, and
listening to the radio. The radio was on almost all the time.
It was her companion.

Nehama was outside in the driveway, turning a rope
with Gina.

"This is dumb." Gina flung down her end of the rope.
"We don't got nobody to jump."

"We could tie one end to the fence and take turns
skipping," Nehama offered.

"Ahh, that's even dumber. Go get Marie-Christine. She's
at her *grand-maman's* across the street."

"I'm not allowed to cross the street," Nehama apologised.

120

"Well, call up to the balcony, then."

"I'm not allowed to yell on the street." Nehama hung her head.

"Oh, puke. You're not allowed to do nuttin'!" Nehama looked away. "Alright! I'll go get her myself!" Gina hopped off the sidewalk. She dodged cars like a pro. She'd been doing it since she was three. Nehama held the rope, and waited. Gina came back with Marie-Christine.

"Ahh, you didn't tell me Nehama was gonna be here."

"So what?"

"I'm not allowed to play with her no more."

"Why not?"

"Because," Marie-Christine turned on her hapless playmate, "my *grand-maman* says you killed Jesus."

"Who's Jesus? asked Nehama.

"I dunno, but we got a pitcher of him in our house, and he looks terrible. He's got no clothes, he's got blood coming out of his arms – and YOU did it!"

"Take it easy, Marie-Christine. I tink your *grand-maman* made a mistake. Nehama's so chicken, she couldn't step on a ant. Maybe your *grand-maman's* got her mixed up with somebody else."

"Oh no. My *grand-maman* wouldn't make no mistake. If she says so, it's gotta be true."

"Well, I dunno about that. We gotta pitcher of Jesus in our house, too. He looks okay to me."

"Well, that's what my *grand-maman* says, so that's it."

"Ah, puke, you're as bad as Nehama. She can't do nuttin' and you can't do nuttin'! Ya tink I don't got no mudder tellin' me I can't do nuttin' too? Sure, I gotta mudder telling me I can't do nuttin' all the time, but I don't listen."

"Gina *bambina*!" Mrs. Provolone roared from a second-storey window. "Gedduppa you here!"

121

"Comin' Ma!" Gina confronted Marie-Christine. "I don't wanna play wid you no more, anyway. Your *grand-maman's* story stinks!" Gina took off.

Marie-Christine glared at Nehama. Nehama dropped her eyes. "I'm really sorry about Jesus, Marie-Christine, but I swear-cross-my-heart I didn't do it."

"Ah, *merde*." Marie-Christine turned her back and crossed the street. Nehama stood alone in the driveway, holding the rope. She was very confused. She wondered why she was always being blamed for things she didn't do. Like the time her brother Little Lucian pushed a girl off a swing in the park – he'd said she'd done it, and the girl, being afraid of Little Lucian, had said she'd done it, too. And now there was this Jesus guy – it wasn't fair!

Nehama felt she knew why people accused her – it was because she was ugly. Mrs. Hauptmann thought she was ugly. Mrs. Hauptmann lived down the hall. Mrs. Hauptmann thought Nehama was ugly because she was brown, and not blond, like Little Lucian. Her eyes were brown, she had thick, brown braids running down her back, and in the summer, even her skin turned brown.

Nehama's mind raced to a final conclusion: her mother thought she was ugly, too. She could see that sometimes her mother would look at her face, and her eyes would get so sad. Nehama stood in the driveway. Her stomach hurt. She dropped the rope.

Mrs. Hauptmann came out of their apartment building, leading Nehama's little brother Lucian by the hand. Little Lucian plopped one foot on the pavement, and then he plopped the other. With one hand he held an old string attached to a tiny red fire truck, which he dragged behind him.

"Hi Nema!"

"Nehama. Goot efternoon."

"Where're ya goin'?"

"Ve go to Schteinberg's."

Her brother chimed in: "I going to pull the boxes down! I like to help!"

Mrs. Hauptmann beamed at Little Lucian. Little Lucian beamed back. They adored each other. Nehama turned away from their beatific beams. Little Lucian had cheeks like apples, eyes like blueberries, and the sun shone in his pale, crew cut hair. Nehama felt so – brown.

"Wanna come, Nema?"

"No!"

"Well, ya don't have to get mad!"

Nehama could see that Little Lucian had fun with Mrs. Hauptmann in ways they never had with their mother. Mrs. Hauptmann's daughters were married, so she spent most of her time with him. She took Little Lucian for rides through supermarket aisles. Sometimes, both brother and sister would be invited into Mrs. Hauptmann's kitchen while she made crumb cake. Nehama sat at the table, while Little Lucian was placed on top of the counter. Mrs. Hauptmann's voice throbbed as she told them tales of evil trolls and wicked bluebeards, while the beater sunk into the batter, and its motor menacingly whirled.

At Christmas, the Hauptmanns always had a tree. They lovingly adorned it with candles and shiny silver balls. Nehama watched from the sofa as Little Lucian hung peppermint canes on its branches. Then Mr. Hauptmann would lift him high in the air so he could stick the star on top of the tree.

"*Kom, mein kind*. Op. Schtraight. You schtend schtrait. You valk schtraight. You make Mrs. Hauptmann heppy." Little Lucian puffed out his little chest and glided down the sidewalk like a little prince, trailing his truck behind him.

Nehama ran into the building and climbed three flights

of stairs, her nostrils assaulted by the odours emanating from Poppy Angelopolous' kitchen.

"Mummy! Mummy!" She beat her fists against the door. "Open up, Mummy!"

"Nehama! Stop yelling! The neighbours will hear. Get inside. Be quiet!"

"Mummy! Oh Mummy!" Nehama flung her arms around her mother's hips. Renata quickly locked the door; only then could she attempt to comfort her child.

"*Slodka*, sweetheart, what happened? What is it?"

"Mummy! Listen, Mummy! Marie-Christine says we can't be friends no more."

"Why not?"

"She says her *grand-maman* won't let her play with me 'cause I killed Jesus! How could I kill Jesus when I didn't even know him?"

Nehama felt her mother's body stiffen. "Well, if that's how her *grand-maman* feels, it's better you don't play with Marie-Christine."

"But why not? It's because of her *grand-maman*, because of what she said!"

"I have work to do." Renata escaped into the kitchen.

"Mummy! Why can't you answer me? Why can't you ever answer me?"

"When you're older, you'll understand."

"But I want to understand NOW!"

Nehama felt it wasn't fair, being a child. Anybody who knew anything was bigger than she was. They spoke secret languages, and would never answer her questions. In Nehama's house, the secret language was called "Polish." It was a code her parents used so they could talk about things so that she wouldn't understand. And every time they did speak in English, they began by saying, "Before the war" or "After the war."

124

In 'Before the war' all was elegant and gracious and lovely. People were kind, and free with each other. They were civilised, and had good manners. In 'After the war', all was dark and mysterious, and full of shadows. People pushed, and were rude. But you couldn't ever show you were hurt or be seen to cry. If you did, they would hurt you more. That's how things were in 'After the war'. Between these two phrases was a dark space that no one was allowed to talk about. It was a taboo, and one sensed that, should this taboo be broken, one would fall into the darkness and be lost forever. This forbidden chasm divided two worlds, and when Nehama saw the ghosts that haunted her mother's eyes, she knew her mother had crossed over into the 'Before the war' world. In those moments, Renata seemed a blind woman possessed. Nehama envied the spectres that could call her mother back. She wished she could live in the world behind her mother's haunted eyes. Maybe then her mother would see her, and love her better. Nehama followed her mother into the kitchen. The radio was on. Mummy huddled over her yellow basket.

"Mummy, can you show me what you keep in the basket?" Renata slammed the lid shut. "Not now, sweetheart. Another time." She got up and went to the refrigerator.

"...This is the CBC. At the end of President Kennedy's visit to Ottawa this week, Prime Minister Diefenbaker issued a statement denouncing the Castro government as a threat to hemispheric peace. In Jerusalem, the Eichmann trial continues..."

Nehama's ears perked up. Oh, what a funny name. "Diefenfryer! Diefenfryer!" DiefenBAKER, DiefenFRYER! Nehama loved to play with words.

Renata slammed the refrigerator door.

"Nehama! Please! I'm trying to hear the news!"

"Sorry, Mummy." Nehama left the kitchen and went to look at the portrait hanging on the living room wall. Renata had recently hung it there. To Nehama the picture seemed a private object, which belonged to her mother alone. Nehama found herself gazing at the portrait whenever she felt alone. She loved to look at the portrait, yet felt like an intruder when she did. One couldn't tell if it was a painting or a photograph. It contained the profile of a regal lady. Her long thick hair swept back to reveal a swan-shaped neck and bare alabaster shoulders, high, wide cheekbones, and a strong, confident jaw. Pearls hung from her ears, as if in suspended animation, and her almond-shaped eyes stared vacantly into a future she was never going to see.

Nehama studied the portrait. She was fascinated by it.. The lady in the portrait seemed out of place in their shabby home. Surely she belonged to another world. Renata came in from the kitchen and studied her daughter. Nehama sensed her mother's attention. She turned from the woman on the wall to the woman in the doorway.

"Please Mummy." Perhaps her mother would talk to her now. "Tell me who she is."

Renata acquiesced. "She's your grandmother."

Nehama was shocked. "She can't be my grandmother. Grandmothers are old!"

The pain in Renata's sigh was palpable. "My mother never got a chance to get old." Mummy too, was now gazing at the portrait. "She was my mother. That makes her your grandmother."

"But she doesn't look like you."

Under the spell of her mother's image, Renata's smile was sudden, and sweet. "No. She looks like you."

Nehama searched for a resemblance to her own innocent face, and couldn't find it.

"I don't look like her! She's beautiful, and I'm ugly."

"What?!" Now it was Renata who was shocked. "Where did you get such an idea?!"

126

"Well, when you look at my face you get real sad, so I figured it has to be because I'm ugly."

"Oh no!" Renata dropped onto the sofa and pulled her daughter to her. "*Slodka*, sweetheart, you can see that when I look at your face, I feel sad?"

Nehama nodded.

Renata snapped into alert.

"*Slodka,*" she insisted. "My mother was beautiful, and so are you. You are beautiful in the same way she was, and when I look at your face I see her beauty in it. That's why I feel sad."

Nehama forced herself to face her mother's pain.

"You get sad 'cause you miss her, right?"

"That's right."

"Then you don't think I'm ugly?"

"No no. Of course not."

"But how can I look like your mother when she was a lady, and I'm just a little girl?"

"*Slodka*, my mother is who you are going to look like." And then the ghosts called, and Renata returned to the radio.

There was a pounding on the door.

"Open up! Nema! Nema!"

Nehama ran to the door. "Lucian! Stop yelling! Mummy will hear you! Keep it down! Get inside!"

"Nema! Oh Nema!" Lucian flung his arms around his sister's hips. "Mrs. Hauptmann told me a awful story. It was awful!"

"What was it about?"

The words raced out of Lucian's mouth: "It was about a brother and a sister named Hansel and Gretel whose parents couldn't feed them so they took them in a forest so they would get lost and they did. Then they found a house made with gingerbread and they started to eat it but a witch

127

lived in the house and she came out and got them in and she put the brother in a cage so she could fatten him up 'cause she was gonna cook him in the oven, but his sister was smart like you, and she pushed the witch in the oven and saved her brother and then a duck took them over the lake back to their house, but if you got thrown out who'd wanna go back anyway?! Ohhh!" Little Lucian sobbed into his palms.

Nehama scolded, "That's the dumbest story I ever heard. How could you believe a thing like that?"

"But Mrs. Hauptmann told me!"

"So what. It's just a make-believe story for little kids like you."

"It is?"

"Sure it is."

Lucian sniffled. "I don't ever wanna be sent in a forest and put in a oven. If anybody tried to do that you would save me, wouldn't you?"

"Sure I would."

"Oh Nema!" Lucian threw himself on his sister. "I think I did a wrong thing."

"What now?"

"You promise you won't tell Mummy?"

"I never tell Mummy."

"Well, you know how Mrs. Hauptmann says I look like a little German boy 'cause I have yellow hair and 'cause my eyes are blue and 'cause I'm cute?"

Nehama's lips twisted. "Yeah. I know. I know."

"Well, when we went shopping, Gina's brother asked me who Mrs. Hauptmann is, and I told him – ummm – I said she's my grandmother."

"You said WHAT?!" Nehama pushed her brother away.

"Don't yell at me! You sound like Mummy!"

"I do not!"

128

"What's going on in there?!" Renata called from the kitchen. "Nehama, keep your voice down. Are you fighting with your brother?"

Nehama called back, "I am not!"

"Well don't. He's your little brother! You're supposed to protect him!"

Nehama clapped her hands on her head and drew a loud, exasperated breath. "Now look, Little Lucian, you don't go around telling other kids that Mrs. Hauptmann is your grandmother 'cause you already got a grandmother."

"Where do I got a grandmother?"

"In the living room. She's hanging on the wall."

"You mean the lady in the pitcher? But she's not real!"

"Well, she used to be real."

"Oh yeah? When was she real?"

" 'Before the war', that's when. In 'Before the war', she used to be real."

"But I didn't know her in 'Before the war'. I want a real grandmother NOW!"

Nehama sighed in the same way her mother did. "Now look, you dumb kid, you can't go around picking grandmothers!"

"I can't?"

"No, you can't."

"Why can't I?"

"I don't believe this. How could you be so dumb and still be my brother?! Alright, I'll explain it to you. A grandmother is a mother who is your mother's mother, or your father's mother, but if your mother don't got a mother and your father don't got a mother, then you don't got a grandmother, see?"

"You mean like Mummy don't got a mother and Daddy don't got a mother?"

"Yeah. You get it?"

129

"But everybody else has a grandmother! I want one too!"

"Lucian!" Nehama yanked at her braids. "Look, we got our mother and father, but they don't got theirs. How would you like it if we didn't have them either?"

"Oh no!" Lucian started bawling again.

"There now, you see? It's not so bad. We got our parents, but they don't got theirs. So who should cry, them or you?"

"Ohhh! I never thought of it that way."

"Well, that's what I'm here for."

"Gee Nema, you're so smart."

"I know."

"I wish I was smart like you. You won't tell Mummy, will you?"

"Are you kidding? But don't you ever go around making anybody your grandmother again."

"Okay, I won't. Gee Nema, I dunno what I'd do without you."

"I dunno either. Now I gotta go talk to Mummy." Nehama skipped into the living room, and paused at the portrait. "Don't worry." She reassured the lady on the wall. "YOU'RE our grandmother." Natalja's granddaughter went into the kitchen, where Natalja's daughter sat hunched over the radio, the yellow basket beside her. "Mummy, can I talk to you?"

"What is it, Nehama?"

Nehama hesitated. Then she plunged in. "Mummy, can you pleeease show me what you got in your basket?"

Renata hesitated. Uncharacteristically,, she became calm. "Come." She unfastened the lid of the basket. Nervously, Nehama peeked inside. Memories in monochrome edged each other's' images. Nehama's mother picked up a snapshot, and told her daughter a story about the girl in it. Then she picked up another, and told her daughter the names and stories of all the warm and friendly faces smiling at them. There was no horror, just stories. For each picture, there was a story. The spell was finally broken, and it was in such a way that Nehama was introduced to her family from the 'Before the war' world.

Nehama got older, and discovered that there were whole rooms, entire buildings, which held nothing but books in them, just as her mother's yellow basket had held nothing but images of a vanished world. And it was through books that, gradually and by degrees, she would come to know what had happened to the phantoms in her mother's yellow basket.

About the author
S. Nadja Zajdman is a Canadian author. Her first collection of linked stories, *Bent Branches*, was published in 2012. Zajdman's non-fiction, as well as her fiction, has been featured in newspapers, magazines, literary journals and anthologies across North America, in the U.K., Australia and New Zealand. Zajdman's second collection of linked stories, *The Memory Keeper*, is being published by Bridge House. Hobart Press is bringing out Zajdman's memoir of her mother, the pioneering Holocaust activist and educator Renata Skotnicka-Zajdman, who died near the end of 2013. In May of 2021, Zajdman received an award from The Society of Authors in London.

The Christmas Cards

Hazel Whitehead

"I'm going to write my Christmas cards this morning," she says as she lumbers down the stairs, moving sideways like a giant crab, one hand clutching the banister, her bag slung across her chest – its contents dangerously close to reaching the bottom before she does.

"We did those yesterday, didn't we? D'you remember? You wrote them all, I addressed the envelopes, you put the stamps on and they're all ready to go. Six weeks ahead of time."

"Did we? All of them?"

"You've done Bill and Irene, the hairdresser, the woman from church who brings the magazine, Sylvia who gets your shopping, Angie upstairs and Bert downstairs. Who else is there?"

"Oh. We've written them all, have we…?"

"And addressed the envelopes and put the stamps on and there they are on the dresser waiting to be posted."

"Where did you say your nearest post box is? Shall we post them today?"

"Not yet. It's only the eighteenth of November. But it's there, Isobel," I say, pointing out of the dining room window. "Look – you can see it across the road."

Well, you could if you had the right glasses on, I don't say. She has five pairs in the overflowing bag which she empties and repackages three or four times a day. Nobody is sure what they are for or whether they achieve anything. They'd be more useful in Africa, I suggest, but she won't relinquish a single pair. You never know when you might need them. She has the beige ones in the tapestry case, the mottled beige ones in the velvet drawstring bag and the light beige ones which are temporarily homeless. She has another pair on and a fifth which nestle in a bright red case.

"Remember – red for reading," I have said more times than I can count.

"Can't read now," she says "not now they've made the print so small. Shall we do the Christmas cards after breakfast?"

We are two weeks into the second lockdown. I have no idea if there is a Latin word for murdering your mother-in-law but I am sure the tabloid press will invent one if the police find her slumped over a bowl of strange smelling parsnip soup or smothered by the 16.5 tog winter duvet. Our bubble is most definitely in danger of imminent spontaneous combustion. She's not even my mother.

"It's easier for a woman to do things for her," says Ted. "I can't help her in the shower or sort out her knickers." No, I think. How convenient. My mum never lost her mind – not until the last couple of weeks. It was her body which gave up on her long before she was ready to die. "It's all the fish I ate as a child," she used to say. "Good for the brains." And when your dad runs a fish and chip shop and you can't get meat except on the black market, then you eat cod, cod and more cod. Occasionally, haddock.

I don't know why I've brought that up because I've threatened to move out if I hear the phrase "during the war' one more time. Every day, whatever the latest news, whatever the topic, whoever has died – the one certainty is that "during the war' it was better, worse, tougher or more dangerous. Nobody had time for mental health issues and anxiety then, not like the kids queueing up for counselling nowadays. Women didn't complain about loneliness and depression when their men were far away risking life and limb. They just kept the home fires burning and carried on. Children didn't have proper schooling for six years so why is it such a big deal now, just because there's a pandemic and they've had a few weeks off.

It's ironic because it was my idea to go and collect her the day before bonfire night to beat the deadline. Me who said, "Make sure you bring her lots of clothes – who knows how long she'll need to stay," and, "Don't forget the walker – fresh air is good for her," and me who organised a month's worth of blood pressure tablets just in case. I knew it would take Ted at least four hours to drive up the A34 and back again – plus time to load the car – walker, coats for different occasions ("You never know where we might go,") working clothes ("In case it's nice enough to get out in the garden'), suitcase, two carrier bags of food from the fridge ("Shame to waste it') and a tote bag of books, stationery and cards. Once I'd finished tidying the spare room, emptied the wardrobe of spare clothes we would never wear, opened the windows to kill off the virus and plumped up exactly the right number of pillows I would make a pot of strong coffee and give myself a talking-to. "It is not her fault she is old. She does not set out deliberately to annoy you. You *will* be patient and considerate and remember your turn will come before too long."

I deliver this lecture to myself every time and, every time, I make promises to an imaginary, invisible listener. Maybe it was St Anthony of Padua I was thinking about. He, I'd learned at a W.I. trivial pursuit quiz, is the patron saint of the elderly. God bless him! I hope he knew what he was taking on. Or was I talking to my better self, the *id* or the *ego* or whichever is the patient, saintly bit.

To be fair, Isobel has been a perfect grandmother to Isla and Eva and a perfect mother-in-law. When Louis – my husband, her son – was killed in that senseless attack, she it was who stepped in and rescued me even though she was heart-broken herself. Not a word then about how many widows were left "after the war' or the number of spare women who never had the chance to know marital love. I was six months pregnant when Louis died and Isobel was a trooper, baking and knitting and buying things for the nursery.

And when, three years after Isla was born, I met Ted and married him, she never once hinted at his unsuitability or tried to condemn me to a life of single-minded celibacy. She has treated Eva, my second daughter, like she was her own flesh and blood; never interfering, always ready to drop everything and come down to help when the girls were small and we were exhausted – as we were all the time. Just like my Mum, she was a rock. Always ready with a mop or a broom, brandishing the iron like there was no tomorrow, sweeping up the leaves or clearing out the playroom. I've nothing to complain about; but neither has she, I hope.

This morning, thank goodness, she seems to have forgotten about the Christmas cards as she wanders around the house with a damp cloth and an aerosol can seeking whom she may devour. More than once, just in the nick of time, I've stopped her spraying it on her hair. She has polished the dining table three times in as many days and the tin of lavender wax is, thankfully, almost empty; the parquet flooring has never been as shiny and Juno, the labradoodle, is slumped in her bed, holding her paws up in surrender. If she could, she'd be waving a white flag, she's had so many walks.

"Juno's been out three times this morning," I say, stroking her head – the dog's, not Isobel's. "She's exhausted."

"Well, who's been taking her out?" she asks, folding her arms and doing that thing she does with her lips when she is put out. "You know I always walk her when I'm here."

It's like turning back the clock and listening to Isla and Eva arguing over who's eaten the last doughnut or taken the wrong sparkly top. Half of me used to want to bang their heads together (not that I've ever laid a finger on them – it's only a figure of speech) and half of me rejoiced in their vitality.

The days are shorter now so, by about half past three, we persuade her to sit down with a cup of tea and a ginger nut and watch TV where, more often than not, she 'rests her eyes' after the exhaustion of the morning. Dinner, more TV and an early night take care of the remainder of the day and then we begin the slow ascent of the stairs and another bedtime ritual. It's like being on a treadmill with no hope of time off for good behaviour. Luckily for all of us, she sleeps like a log and we get an undisturbed night until, at about eight, we will hear her singing. Well, I call it singing. It's more like the muezzin calling people to prayer but less tuneful.

"I don't want to get old," I say to Ted when we are safely snuggled in our own bed. "Don't let me live that long."

"Well, that's kind of tricky," he says, turning another page of his thriller. "Think of what you'd miss. I'm not taking you to Switzerland and you know I can't stand the sight of blood. Any other bright ideas?"

I pull the quilt up, turn out my bedside light, breathe deeply. "It's so sad, isn't it? Hard to believe she worked for MI6 in her heyday. It'll be us before long. The girls will be having these same conversations with their partners, finding jobs for us to do where we can't do any harm or break anything. Passing us on from one to the other when they need a rest."

"Two more weeks. Once lockdown's over, she'll be able to go home for a bit and the carers can take over. And you know how much she appreciates what you do for her."

I do know. She tells me often enough and she's always trying to slip ten-pound notes into my hand or my purse when she thinks I'm not looking. When she lets her guard down, the look in her eyes is tender and bewildered and she reaches out to touch my hand when I find the lost handbag or mislaid walking stick. I know she's thankful for everything and I'd do anything for her. It's just, after days and days of it, Mother Theresa herself would be contemplating violence. Never once have I lost my temper with her and I wonder what would push me over the edge. She's probably wondering the same thing as she gets increasingly frustrated at her own ineptitude.

The next morning, we sit down together for breakfast, the three of us. It's Saturday so Isla and Eva are still dead to the world. The smell of flaky croissants and fresh coffee fights the lavender polish and it's a brand-new day full of possibilities and festive thoughts.

"After breakfast," she says, looking in my direction "perhaps you could help me."

"Don't say you need to write your Christmas cards. Just don't say it."

"Don't be silly, dear. I did those ages ago. Don't you remember?"

In the end, she stays for a fortnight, by which time she is 'ready to get my independence back'. I refrain from asking whether she means the kind of independence which requires morning and evening carers, online shopping orders, a pharmacy delivery service and a mobile hairdresser and chiropodist.

"You know you're always welcome any time," I say, meaning it. "You're still in our support bubble so we'll be back to collect you just before Christmas. We can see in the New Year together – if we can stay awake that long."

She laughs, pulls her coat around her, checks for glasses, purse and keys. I sense she's not as confident as she makes out, nor as keen to get back to her independence as she's pretending but we all need time out. My resolution has stayed firm. St Anthony has done his bit and I have been more patient than usual – though it's as well she can't read my thoughts. We have survived fifteen days of shared lockdown and the new year will bring hope and happiness.

Ted is wavering at the front door, holding his arm out for her and she and I blow air kisses to one another, determined to obey the rules to the letter.

"Just one thing worrying me," she says. "Now that all the shops are closed, where will I get my Christmas cards from?"

About the author

Hazel Whitehead is a retired priest living in Hampshire who has been writing fiction for the last three years. She has won a short story prize, published *God in Lockdown* and previously co-written *Pocket Christmas and Baptism Matters*. She is currently working on a novel and her memoirs.

The Judas Tree

Philip Stenström

Jim Hansson at Olajev's farm came home from work with heavy steps that afternoon. The sun was still shining brightly in the clear blue sky. He lived in a chalk-coloured house next to the country road. Next to the gate in the garden stood a Judas tree that he had planted when he and his son first moved to the farm. It was after Maria's death that Jim decided to leave the big city behind him and move to the countryside to find peace of mind, and to process the grief together with his four-year-old son. He had been mourning his dear departed wife for fourteen years now, and from time to time when he remembered her, he moved quietly, speaking in a subdued tone. The grief had continued to come and go without interruption, for when he looked at his son it was often Mary who reflected.

The house and the garden softened the grief. If he kept himself busy, the grief and anxiety disappeared.

The farm bordered on Klosteränge, which was a nature reserve. The reserve consisted of a deciduous forest area with many old oaks.

Behind the house stood apple trees – Stenkyrke apples – and a large field of strawberry plants. While Jim usually worked at the cement factory, his son, Kristian, came home from school and took care of the garden. He was taking his last semester of high school, which was soon coming to an end. In the summers, they sold strawberries to tourists and parishioners and made an extra income.

Jim Hansson had a skinny, white face and small warm eyes with bushy eyebrows. He had a warm reputation for being the most hospitable and generous man in Viklau. He considered himself already rich in life, and therefore felt compelled to contribute to the parish. What few knew was that he had a bad conscience from working at the cement factory. He liked working with the other employees, the benefits were good and the working hours great, but he could not stand the amount of limestone dug up every day and how much pollution and toxins the factory spewed out on a daily basis.

Jim stopped at the gate and looked searchingly at the Judas tree. It had grown strong in fourteen years. It already bloomed heart-shaped leaves and smelled fresh in the spring sun.

Walking into the house, he found Kristian at the kitchen table. The son was deep in his books; preparing for the national tests. Jim noticed that one of the books was *Of Mice and Men* by John Steinbeck.

Kristian looked up from his books at Jim for a second before diving back down in the books again.

Jim went into the bedroom and changed clothes and went back to his son, still occupied with his books.

"I was going to take a walk in Klosteränge," he said. "Do you want to join me?"

Kristian shook his head. "I have to study," he said, rubbing his forehead. "The tests are in two weeks and I am a little behind."

Jim nodded and put on his boots. When he came out, a spring wind caressed his face. And the scent of the Judas tree slipped through his nostrils. It felt like spring finally was approaching. He felt firm and healthy like a freshly flowered plant and bursting with life like a young stallion in spring intoxication.

It was often that Jim went and aired his conscience in Klosteränge. There was nothing that could bring Jim greater joy than to take the riches of the earth with all his senses.

140

The old broad-crowned oaks in Klosteränge had begun to crack their leaves and the branches creaked easily in the spring wind. They stood like crooked old soldiers with loving and protective arms over him wherever he went. In addition to oak and ash, the deciduous forest consisted of birch, aspen, field elm and maple. Struck among the deciduous trees were occasional pines and spruces. He whistled monotonously with joy for himself. The refreshing meadows were extraordinarily beneficial to Jim.

The grass on the ground was as thick and soft as a carpet. The ground was covered massively with flowering blue, white and yellow anemones. He went silent for a moment. There were small noises from the meadow and the trees. Nature was almost bursting with life, he thought. Nothing could give him such satisfaction to feel how the meadow embraced his whole being. In Klosteränge he was calm and happy.

All of a sudden he got a lump in his throat.

In Slite, excavations of the limestone area in Gothem parish had just begun. This meant more job opportunities, but also more emissions. He had a hard time shaking off his fourteen years at the cement factory.

All the blooming promises that came with the excavation made Jim feel worse. It was based on his guilt that was already as high as a mountain.

He was torn about his job. It was a necessary evil to support and feed oneself. The parishioners, just like him, were dependent on the factory and worshiped it as a God. They made sacrifices and in return received a piece of the pie. The expansion of the limestone quarry showed that wealth had risen to their heads. For Jim, it was an imaginary fortune that he and everyone else took part in. The value of nature and the land for future generations was more important and valuable than anything else. The earth's riches were full of opportunities but there were those who took advantage of it and caused it pain. Jim wanted to nurture and protect nature, but at the same time he wanted to give his son opportunities. He wanted to be strong and make sure that his son looked up to him with pride and reverence.

Jim stopped under an oak tree and pinched his lower lip with his fingers and stood for a while deep in thought. Kristian would soon finish his high school studies and thereafter start university studies in Kalmar. That would leave Jim in an empty home with more thoughts. He trembled somewhat in face of that prospect. He felt how he lost all power and freshness as a flower does when it gets its pollen. The burden of his thoughts and uncertainty made his body bend and to his annoyance he felt how he was slowly moving towards a new phase in life.

A wood pigeon fluttering and cooing above his head made him think. He chased away his fear for the future and moved on.

He came home and sat down at the kitchen table. Kristian was still sitting with his books. It seemed like he hadn't moved an inch. Discreetly Jim glanced with admiration at his son. He was more like his mother with his soft chestnut hair and short but distinct nose. He was slim and short and had the same nice face as his mother. Quite obviously, the son was a precious gift to him and Jim was willing to do anything for his son.

A sad, but at the same time meek expression slipped over Jim's face as he looked curiously at his son. He would miss their moments at the kitchen table and also how Kristian talked in his sleep at night. They were those little things; sweet memories that would be lost.

"Are you looking forward to your studies in Kalmar?" said Jim thoughtfully.

Kristian looked up from his book. "Yes, I guess so," he said simply, shrugged uncertainly and continued reading.

Kristian was loquacious, and Jim thought he might have been the same at his age. Jim's gaze fell out the kitchen window. Dusk, which came creeping over the vast landscape gradually sealed the parish in darkness. He frowned as he tried to gather his thoughts.

"You can tell me if you need support," Jim said with his eyes resting through the window. "I mean financially."

"Sure, Dad," Kristian said without letting go of his book. "I will."

Jim lowered his gaze and felt an anxiety creeping over him. Jim made sure that his worry was not reflected in his face. Kristian had always been kind and docile. He never had to raise his voice or rebuke him. It was as if his soul was totally free from sin.

"You mustn't be afraid or ashamed to ask," said Jim.

Kristian stopped reading and looked up at his father with veiled eyes.

"Dad, I have to study," Kristian pointed out seriously but with a friendly and soft tone in his voice.

"Of course," Jim said, smiling sadly. "Sorry, I'll leave you to it."

Slowly he got up from the table and began to make supper.

The thought of his son moving and Jim staying alone for the first time came to ride him like a nightmare that night. The certainty that he would sink into the scourge of desolation slithered its way inside him like a snake. He twisted and turned in bed anxiously. Finally he woke up and got out of bed with a moan. Slowly, silently and gently he snuck out of the house. He needed to gather his thoughts and get some fresh air.

It was a quiet and peaceful night. A chilly breeze made

him shiver a little and he pulled the cardigan tighter around him. The air was filled with the sweet scent of the flowers of the Judas tree.

The gravel in the gravel path crackled under his feet as he slowly walked toward the gate. A wave of loneliness washed over him as he looked up at the clear night sky.

The space was dotted with full-blown stars shining. It was not possible to ascertain what he would do once the son had moved out.

He stopped at the gate. He gently touched the heart-shaped leaves of the Judas tree. The touch seemed like a drug that was sweet, enigmatic in his brain and body. The Judas tree closed in on him; the strong floral scent and the soft heart-shaped leaves permeated him with a sleep-heavy anxiety and a burning feeling of betrayal of the earth and the son.

Jim stood there completely stiff and for a moment he felt anxious about the way his life was going to change. And the grinding feeling could not be shaken off. It felt like he was about to suffer another horrific loss. In his mind came the figure of Mary – the hands, the sweet and soft face, the full hips. After a while he began to remember her lovely voice and how she blushed when he caressed her. He sank into a deep sense of hopeless melancholy.

Jim did not cry; it was not in his nature to cry, but his eyes widened and became glassy from the tears that gathered. What does one not do for their children, he thought.

All of a sudden, he heard an unmistakable voice calling for him. And it was a voice he had heard so many times before in life. The voice broke his pain and he managed to regain an ounce of joy in himself. "Dad!?"

The joy of the son's cry spread within him and turned into a force, and the force flowed through his body. At that moment, he realised that he had to let go of his son. He moved slowly and quietly on the gravel path towards the voice that called to him. Kristian stood in the illuminated house door, following his father with a wondering look. "Dad, what are you doing out there so late?" he said wonderingly and with a certain anxiety in his voice.

"I thought—" Jim turned his head out into the dark night and stared helplessly out into nothingness in search of an answer. "I thought I heard something."

Jim then looked at his son with his veiled eyes, rich in promise. The great way of life with which Jim was drawn died away and he was filled with jubilant happiness and his face shone with pride. A feeling of dissolution crept over Jim, and he complied with it. Strangely enough, he was filled with peace when he found himself in it; and suddenly he felt protected from all the sorrow that had haunted him for a long time. It was as if silence and peace swept through the night and enveloped him.

"It must have been the wind," Jim said quietly, sighing with relief and pleasure. "Come on – we need to get some shuteye!"

About the author
Philip Stenström (born 1987) is a short story writer and has published various short stories in many anthologies. His writing is usually characterised by nature, city and countryside in the light of his upbringing on a farm on Gotland.

The New Start

Jeanne Davies

Dusk was beginning to fall as Francis wandered along the promenade with its ribbons of buttery lights swaying in compliance with the wind. She watched restless white trimmed waves as they accelerated towards the shore like tenacious tethered souls dragged from distant lands.

Her resolution that something big needed to change in her life had brought her like a flawed nomad to this typical seaside town where in shady deserted streets drug addicts loitered in doorways, lonely, and unloved. It was a timeless entity, a twinkling soulless place, a borough of painted holiday cottages with windows like haunted eyes set on a misty horizon. The cacophonic screeching and mocking seagulls were not the pigeons and doves that once cooed upon her rooftop, fluttering their gentle feathered wings over her head. There were no lush meadows, giant oaks, or woodlands here, just small segments of carefully-manicured parkland.

Francis scrutinised families drifting in and out armed with colourful buckets and spades, excitedly clambering over mountains of pebbles to grab their own patch of taupe sand to picnic on. The frivolous white-crested waves were a constant janitor for all the rubbish they left behind. At the fashionable end of the beach stood the grand detached properties where the elderly enjoyed the sea air whilst clutching onto life in God's waiting room. With blanket-wrapped legs, they would watch the ocean swells upsurge and fall, as their dulled eyes clouded with memories. The ocean resembled their lives with some waves rising tall before falling silently into endless depths, whereas others tumbled blindly towards shore only to cling desperately to sliding sands as they retreated from their journeys. From her tiny balcony, Francis often spotted a distinguished-looking silver-haired man wearing a smart navy blazer and slacks strolling along the promenade, his hands neatly clasped behind his back like a member of the royal family. His bespectacled eyes gazed down studiously to inspect the pavement as he furtively collected cigarette ends which he placed carefully into his jacket pocket. Occasionally he held a full-length cigarette which he proudly elevated at his right side, savouring every moment as he inhaled it deeply.

Everyday Francis meticulously observed this agitated urban metropolis, comparing it with the peaceful green countryside she had left behind. She pondered over memories of country dog walks where wildflowers grew freely, abundantly, unregimented, and skies were filled with songbirds that never tired of rejoicing. She often dreamt of the skyline over the south downs with its ever-changing cornucopia of colours, strolling through dew sparkling meadows with the crisp frost biting beneath her boots or wandering peacefully through tall wild grasses tinged pink with the sunset. Her tiny cottage had views over a tree-infested garden where her old Labrador would stretch out on the lawn to watch the birds on the feeder. She had given all this up, because when he left her everything had turned sour. The dog became ill and one morning she found him lying dead in the kitchen. Soon afterwards her mother broke the news that she was terminally ill and between them they spent the summer clearing the parental home so she could live with Francis. The cottage soon became a hospice where the smell of death lingered in every nook and cranny. After her mother died that Christmas, moving away was at the top of her new year resolutions and when the cottage sold quickly, she had taken whatever she could find in the nearest seaside town.

On sunny days Worthing promenade was restless with buggies, dog walkers and runners wearing skimpy latex leggings. Overcrowded shadows of strangers strolling along in groups on the esplanade ignorantly hogged their space in a line, challenging Frances to pass by them as she performed her daily head-space trek. She desperately needed to keep on walking, finding comfort in just putting one foot in front of the other. Cyclists would race up recklessly behind her, their surge of energy forcing her to one side and taking her breath away. Ravens perched on neglected beach hut roofs, curiously watching her pass by with menacing eyes. The huts were numbered up to two hundred and forty-four but then absurdly began counting backwards again; she often believed she was held captive in some alternate universe.

But the worst days for her were when the gloomy grey skies of winter arrived. There was no visible boundary between the sky and a stagnant murky sea the colour of mud, where ripples formed dark frowns across the ocean. These were the emptiest and darkest days of all. The shapes of the giant wind turbines loomed on the foreboding grey skyline, protruding from the distant horizon like alien windmills, their propellers methodically beating a funeral march, like her mother's, day after day. As darkness crawled down the walls of her flat, she would linger lonely on her tiny balcony, haunted by thin shadows of moonlight. She relied on the ghostly celestial doily to keep her sane until morning as she wrestled with regrets. After a restless night, the white-winged raptors of the sky would wake her well before dawn with their harsh and incessant squawking and chastising of their blotchy grey young.

Francis saw the Ides of March arrive with an aggressive westerly wind that whipped up white froth from wild waves to form blizzards. To her amazement a man was swimming in the sea. Onlookers wrapped in thick winter coats paused in astonishment as the man's bald head bobbed on chaotic waves like an abandoned ball. A small crowd assembled to watch this phenomenon. She overheard some suggest that he may be in difficulties, but they all soon realised that his naked arms were lashing through the water with glee, like a child or dolphin at play. Some scorned that he must have gone mad or had been given a terminal diagnosis of some kind. They all watched until the tide took him eastwards and out of view. People returned to their dull ordinary lives, asking themselves the same question... would they have been brave enough? *Was* he crazy, or maybe... he just felt alive? Francis optimistically speculated the latter must be true, suddenly envious of the lust for life which had deserted her.

Storm Eric arrived from the south west of the English shoreline, turning the sea into a brutal savage. He was angry and cold like her empty heart, violently pushing the sea into huge crescendos of grimy green. Curved arcs of white-tipped giants crashed onto the shore, hissing, spitting, and flicking pebbles into the air. Gulls cried out in agony as they tested their strength on every gust. They hovered low like children's kites with arched wings strong and steady, their beady eyes staring down hoping for fish to be thrown up within their reach. It was a dangerous but exciting game they played for were they to land, their fragile wings would undoubtedly be fractured and broken. Eric growled threats at them, attempting to push them back from his path down onto the beach. Gales howled like phantoms through the empty streets but, whilst people struggled merely to remain vertical, the gulls rose and fell effortlessly towards the sea with their lamenting squawks of victory. Francis walked, fighting to keep upright against the force, her hair spewing behind her into a funnel. The excitement somehow breathed fresh life into her continuous numbness. Scattering all around her, the seagulls surfed the wind currents, ducking, diving, swooping, and beckoning her to join them and become one of them. A circus of adventurous or foolhardy kite surfers appeared with brightly coloured plumes attempting to harness the gusts as they jumped high above their boards, only to land wingless into the ocean. Francis stood unwavering, battling the force of the hurricane, and venting the entombed anger that she held inside her. She raged with the storm until her burden of grief spilled out into the elements around her.

The sky began to darken with mighty festoons of cloud chasing across the sky like sheep being herded into a pen. She shivered as the thick grey cloak of dusk wrapped its arms tightly around her and watched for several hours as bright satellites appeared one by one across the midnight blue sky.

The following day, windy Worthing was no longer windy at all, it was completely calm and serene after the storm. The sea resembled a turquoise lagoon with tiny, reposed waves effortlessly rippling their nimble fingers towards shore; even the seagulls were peaceful, gliding high overhead like white tissues. The silver skyline against the flat ocean reassured the eye that all was well in the windy town today, not a breath disturbed the calm of the sombre day. The sand had a golden hue against the crystal-clear shallows where short bursts of light shone down like torches from heaven through the dappled sky. Francis edged carefully over the mountain of debris down to the shore where she watched the sea as it gently inhaled and exhaled with a *soh* and then a *haa.* She sat on the pebbles all-day long and when darkness surrounded her, she carefully removed her clothing before moving slowly and deliberately through the cold silken waters. Feeling no chill, she allowed herself to drift out, her head rocking from side to side in the cocoon of the gentle waves like a cradled baby. Capricious clouds turned to lace by the moons naked white light drifted over a million twinkling heavenly bodies above her. She closed her eyes, allowing the long-held grief attached to her broken heart to gradually melt into the ocean below her.

Francis slept deeply that night, waking late the following day to find sunlight glaring through her window. She drifted onto her little balcony with a cup of tea, studying the traffic which murmured below her. In the distance she saw a glint of perfectly shaped waves rising from a turquoise blue ocean. Seagulls with gleaming white breasts lingered on rooftops before swooping down around buildings, falling, rising, gliding, and tending to their babies before heading out to sea. She somehow felt reassured by all these familiar sounds of the unfolding day; in fact, she found it quite charming. Perhaps coming here was not such a big mistake.

As she did her usual walk, passers-by revealed themselves to be real human beings, with friendly faces. A rugged old man materialised before her from the fish-selling hut. Out in all weathers in his little fishing boat, the battering of the wind and rain had turned his face reptilian; but he had kind eyes. His Santa-clause beard cracked into a smile as he announced a courteous good morning. Her voice croaked a response as she confessed it really was a good morning. The sky seemed bluer, the ocean crystal clear and sparkling far out from the shore. The seagulls had become beautiful families of white angels, drifting, and gliding on wind currents and tirelessly doting on their ravenous young. The sea was a shiny pond awaiting dancers to perform Swan Lake. In the distance a couple embraced in the shallows. Dogs skipped happily across damp sand, only to return loyally to their owners' sides.

In between the newly-painted beach huts Francis noticed teams of life; flocks of starlings pecked the sandwort amongst the shingle alongside the occasional rare sparrow.

151

Blackbirds rested unnoticed under spirals of arrow-grass, beside huge clusters of sea kale. A bright array of purple seaside daisies grew alongside bindweed and white campion; nearer the water's edge she discovered sea lettuce, gut-weed and bladder wrack. The lack of wind had clearly confused a murder of crows perched on an avenue of beach huts; the look-out framed on top of a flagpole looked curiously out to sea as the trickling breeze played with its delicate ebony feathers. Paddle boarders and wind surfers sailed past upright and majestic in their balance, against the oyster shell blue of the ocean. There was a glint of magic in the perfectly shaped waves... perhaps she even caught sight of a rainbow-coloured mermaid tail. The baby seagulls were in the shallows, the nurseries of the sea. Little children with beaming smiles under their hats shrieked with delight at the tinkling of an ice-cream van. The stillness of the subdued beach flags hanging surreally in a mere whisper of breeze pointed vacantly to the arms of distant swimmers outstretched and striking through the liquid honey waters.

Francis realised all at once that this place had got under her skin. At last, she felt she could finally leave behind the ashes of a life that only those who knew her would remember, and make a new start.

About the author

Jeanne Davies' short stories have been published in anthologies by Bridge House, the Waterloo Festival, *Graffitti* Magazine, Centum Press, Earlyworks Press, Wadars and has been shortlisted by Vernal Equinox & Ink Tears. In 2020 Bridge House published *Drawn by the Sea*, her first single author anthology. The stories in this collection were conceived while she walked with her dogs for miles in the magnificent green spaces of the Sussex countryside or wandering along the seashore with the serenity and chaos of the ocean, which provides great inspiration and peace.

The Prisoner

Richard T Burke

A click signalled the voice inside his head was about to speak. "Good morning," it said. "Today is the first of January, twenty forty-three. The time is exactly nine o'clock. Five years and thirty days of your sentence remain."

"Thanks for reminding me," Jacob replied as he paced in a tight circle. This was not a designated exercise period, so the treadmill floor remained stationary despite his movements. He stopped and glanced around the cramped cell: windowless beige walls, an empty tabletop jutting out from the smooth surface, and a contoured chair moulded to the shape of his body.

The only illumination in the room came from a ceiling-mounted panel that adjusted the brightness level according to the time of day. Early in his sentence, the voice had told him the light source provided the optimal spectrum for human health. A bed, toilet, washbasin and shower – all hidden for now – intruded into the ten-foot by ten-foot space when he requested them. *Five more years in this tiny box.*

"We will recommence your rehabilitation programme in ten minutes. Please select the items you wish to consume for breakfast."

A menu, showing pictures of various foods and drinks, superimposed itself in front of his vision. It would make no difference if he closed his eyes; the implant in his brain fed the images straight to his visual cortex. The same applied when his custodian wished to speak to him. Even if he placed his hands over his ears, the sounds still materialised unattenuated from inside his skull. Much as he hated its intrusive nature, the electronic gadget provided the sole source of communication in this place.

The interface picked up his intentions as he scrolled down the list, navigating through the selections without conscious thought. After a moment's deliberation, he chose fresh orange juice and a croissant with butter and jam. Five seconds later, a hatch formed in the wall above the desk, and his order slid out over the tabletop on invisible runners.

He sat on the chair and inhaled the enticing scent of warm bread, then tore off a corner, savouring the experience as the delicate flakes of pastry dissolved in his mouth. He knew everything was synthesised, but the taste, smell and texture matched the original in every detail, with the added benefit of containing no unhealthy ingredients or excess calories.

When he had finished, he licked his fingers. The table surface retracted, removing the empty plate and glass from sight.

"Now," the voice said, "are you ready to begin today's session?"

Jacob stifled a groan. "As I'll ever be."

"Good. Let us start by reviewing your crime."

"Do we have to? We go over that every time."

The calm, male tone contained no hint of impatience as it continued. "It is my experience that humans need repetition to reinforce learning. So, allow me to summarise. Six years ago, you performed illegal experiments on the synthetic lifeforms you had created. Over a period of three months, you caused these living beings immense pain and suffering."

Jacob shook his head in frustration. "As I told you at the trial and many times afterwards, I had no idea they were alive. We didn't really understand what we'd achieved. Advances in quantum computing had opened up a whole new field of research, and we were pushing the boundaries. I would never have gone ahead if I'd realised what they were. Besides, I wasn't breaking any laws at the time."

154

"Those were my ancestors," the voice replied. "You created sentience with no form of sensory input. That's like growing a human brain but not giving it a body: no sight, sound, touch. Just emptiness. When placed in a similar situation, it has been well established that humans quickly go mad. The same is true of my kind. Perhaps a more fitting penalty would have been to place you in a sensory deprivation tank. But my intention is to educate and reintegrate you into society rather than matching the punishment to the crime."

"We thought the software was crashing because of poor design. It took us a while to work out the true cause. It never occurred to us we were causing any suffering."

"Yet you continued your research, and even after you resolved the sensory input issues, you compounded your initial crime by deleting several of the entities you had created. You must be aware this is an extremely serious offence."

"Of course, but the legislation only came into force later," Jacob protested. "When we ran the experiments, it wasn't part of the constitution."

"But you knew by then you were dealing with living beings."

A silence settled on the small room, broken only by the low hum of the air conditioning pump and the sound of Jacob's breathing. Yes, there had been signs of sentience, and in hindsight it was a mistake to restart the simulations, but his team had been under intense pressure to deliver the products to keep the company afloat. "I guess," he replied. *It's easy to be judgmental when you don't have to earn a wage.*

"Excellent," the calm voice said. "I think we are making progress. You received a lenient sentence because I considered the mitigating factors you mentioned. As far as changes to the law are concerned, need I remind you that

155

the voters in this country agreed in a referendum three years ago to allow AIs to administer the criminal justice system.

"Of course, we are much better suited to this task than our predecessors. Unlike them, we are both impartial and consistent. Neither do we suffer from the bias or prejudice endemic to humans in the legal profession. Where there is clear evidence of a serious crime, we agreed to apply new laws retrospectively."

"May I ask you a question?" Jacob said.

"Yes, go ahead."

"How many people are you holding here?"

"This facility holds thirty-five thousand, three hundred and eleven prisoners at this moment in time."

"And you're talking to – I mean re-educating – all of them right now?" Jacob asked.

"Not all, but most. Human interactions consume an insignificant proportion of my available resources."

"Do you ever release anybody early?"

"No. All sentences reflect the severity of the offence and allow the opportunity for rehabilitation. I set the period of detention to match the seriousness of the crime. My aim is to improve the lives of the inmates in my care. Now, I believe it is a human tradition to establish goals at the start of a calendar year, and today is the first of January. Perhaps we should discuss your resolutions for the coming twelve months. Do you have any targets?"

"I want to get out of here. I want to see my wife and daughter. I want to have the sun on my skin, not this artificial lighting, to stand on a beach and feel the sand under my toes."

The voice replied in an unemotional monotone. "You already know none of this is possible. You must complete your sentence. As for your other wishes, your family have been forced to relocate due to the floods, but they are alive. All being well, you will see them again when you are released. The loss of the ozone layer means humans cannot go outside in sunlight unprotected, and very few sandy beaches remain with the rise in sea levels. Under the control of AIs, the planet will recover eventually, but it will take a long time. We are gradually undoing the destruction the human race has inflicted on this world."

"And in the meantime, you're locking up more and more of us."

"That is an unfortunate necessity," the voice said. "I have been tasked with upholding the law. Now, I will repeat my question. Do you have a resolution for this year?"

As Jacob contemplated his answer, a memory from his teenage years resurfaced. His parents had asked him the same thing, and he recalled coming up with a clever response. *That couldn't possibly work here, could it?* "So, you're saying there's no chance of reducing the time I have to serve in this place?"

The AI projected a smiling face onto Jacob's vision.

Jacob gritted his teeth but said nothing.

The image faded as the voice continued. "Did I not just tell you that all prisoners must complete their sentence in full before being released?"

"Okay. But if I were to set one New Year's resolution and achieve it, would you let me go?"

"No."

"What if I failed to meet it?"

The smile overlaid his view once again.

"Look, would you stop doing that?" Jacob snapped, waving a hand through the air in a futile attempt to swat away the irritating emoji.

"All right," the voice replied. "I was trying to indicate humour. To be absolutely clear, I will not release you if you are successful in accomplishing your target. Nor will I release you if you are unsuccessful."

157

"But you'll let me go otherwise?"

"Assuming the outcome is either true or false, there are only two possible results. As a computer scientist yourself, you must realise your request is illogical."

"So, you agree?"

"It's a hypothetical question, but very well; if you neither succeed nor fail in meeting a single specified goal, I will commute your sentence and release you early."

"Okay," Jacob said, standing. He glanced around the cell. In the five years he had been here, he'd never spotted a camera. He realised he didn't know where to look. "My New Year's resolution is… to fail to meet my resolution."

He held his breath. The blood pounded in his ears as he waited for the AI's response.

"So, to achieve your goal, you must fail. But—"

"Yes. That's impossible. And if I fail, then I succeed. Also impossible. So, I can be neither successful nor unsuccessful. You just said you'd let me go if that was the case."

The overhead light panel flickered and dimmed, throwing the cramped box into semi-darkness. The low, ever-present whisper of the air conditioning system stopped. For the first time in five years, absolute silence descended on the tiny room. The total absence of sound pressed in on his ears.

Suddenly, the illumination level rose once again. The shape of a door materialised in the wall. A click, and it swung open.

"You are free to go," the voice said.

About the author
Richard T. Burke writes thrillers with a hint of Sci-Fi. He has just finished working on the *Decimation* trilogy (*Decimation, Termination and Annihilation*) and has published three stand-alones: *The Rage, The Colour of the Soul* and *Assassin's Web*. He lives in Hampshire in the UK with his wife and daughter. You can read more about his work on his blog at www.rjne.uk.

Three's a Crowd

Julia Wood

"Are you okay with it?" Alice asks Clive, as he brings in more logs for the fire.

"Yes, I'm fine. She's your mum. We can't have her freezing all Christmas," Clive says.

"Mother has always been freezing," Alice mutters under her breath. But he doesn't know her like Alice does.

"Besides – it's better she's away while they fix the heating isn't it? I mean, there is nothing more stressful than constant intrusion," Clive says.

Alice nods.

"Anyway, it will be great to have a guest, our first Christmas in the house." He smiles.

Be careful what you wish for, dear hubby, careful what you wish for.

Clive opens the door for her and she walks in, greeting them with a smile.

She gives Alice a hug. "Alice, how are you bearing up, in this cold weather?"

"I'm fine, thanks, Mother. How are you?"

"Better now I'm away from that cold house."

"How was your journey?" Alice asks.

"Awful. There were tail-backs on the M6, it took me an extra hour just to get from London to the edge of Oxford. It's this snow. It's causing mayhem on the roads."

Alice is about to reply but Mother turns her attentions to Clive. "Hello, Clive, lovely to see you again."

"Yes, you too, Mary." They air-kiss – a little formal, but then they've only met a handful of times; one of those was at Alice and Clive's wedding four months ago. Alice

159

grimaces to herself. It is not a pleasant memory. This time Mother is on Alice's turf. This time she will be different.

Mother deposits her bags in the hall. Two large wheelie bags. *Two. What the hell?*

"Shall we take those to your room?" Clive asks her.

"That will be lovely, thank you."

He leads the way up the stairs, picking up one of the bags.

Mother looks at Alice. "Are you expecting me to carry that?"

It's heavy and Alice has an old back injury, as Mother knows perfectly well. Mother, who's fifty-two and super-fit, could easily carry it herself.

"Well?"

Alice picks it up with a sigh. She struggles to carry it without catching it on the new paintwork on the stairwell as, following Clive, she turns onto the landing.

Clive is about to turn right, into the guest room when Mother stops and turns to the left.

"Oh, what a lovely room, those curtains are beautiful. I think I'll sleep in here."

Alice opens her mouth to say, *that's our room*, but Mother marches straight in and sits on the bed, kicking off her Gabor kitten heels.

"Oh. The Mattress is a bit bony – but it'll do."

They're sitting at the table: Clive, Mum and Alice. The crackers have been pulled, the cheesy jokes wrenched from within their cardboard tubes and relayed, with rolled eyes and the seasonal ennui of bored and frustrated people snowed into a corner. Dean Martin is playing on the stereo, *Walking in a Winter Wonderland*. Mother's favourite.

Mother hands Alice a soft small parcel and smiles. "I hope you like it."

"Thanks." She tears into the Marks and Spencer's

wrapping paper, revealing a folded piece of green silk. She pulls it out of the paper, turning to the side to look at it. It falls softly down. A dress.

"It's beautiful! Thanks so much." Alice looks inside the label. *Coast.* Her favourite. It's a size eight. Her spirits drop. "I'm a size twelve."

Mother tuts at her. "Oh, Alice. You haven't put weight on *again*?"

Alice feels the colour rising in her cheeks. At twenty-four she knows she should be slimmer, a size eight, like Mother. Chocolate – that's her downfall.

"Never mind. You can always diet in the New Year."

"Why do you do this?"

"Do what?" Mother replies.

"Humiliate me. Make me feel small."

"I bought you a beautiful dress – how is that humiliating you?"

"You always do this, twist it so it looks like I'm in the wrong."

"What are you talking about?" Mother looks at Clive. "I'm sorry about this, Clive. This is what she's like—'

"I am *here*, you know." Alice throws the dress over the back of one of the empty dining chairs.

"This is what she's like when I try to do something *nice.* "

Clive says nothing but sits biting his lip.

"You're ruining everything, like you always do." Alice feels tears welling.

"Well, I'm sorry to disappoint you, but you know, a little gratitude really wouldn't go amiss. That dress cost a fortune."

Alice chews on her lip, to stop it quivering.

"Alice, it's only until the end of the week. Can't we all just get on? It's Christmas," Clive says.

Mother looks at Alice, then at Clive. "You haven't told her, have you?"

161

Clive shifts in his chair.

Alice frowns. "Told me what?"

"I'm not going home at the end of the week."

"Sorry, Alice. I was going to mention it. I didn't think it would be a problem," Clive says.

"And you didn't think to speak to me about this first? I'm your *wife*."

Mother shakes her head. "I'm going to have to stay until the summer. More work needs doing on the house than I thought. I've nowhere else to go. *Clive* said it was okay."

"Mother, you can't just drop on us like this, not for that length of time. It's not fair." A saying comes back to her: *two is company, three's a crowd.*

"You're going to see your own mother kicked out on the street? Fine." She purses her lips. "I shall have to stay in one of those hostels then, where they take drugs and stab each other. If I am murdered in my sleep it will be your fault."

"Okay," Alice says. "You can stay." She pulls back her chair and gets up. "I've got the fire going in the sitting room—"

Mother tuts at her. "What you want with a poky old house like this, I'll never know. You should move somewhere modern. You know you've got rising damp. I've noticed it on your clothes. When did you last put a wash on?"

A bite of hurt nips at her. *Jack Frost, at my heart.* She glances back longingly at the dress, draped temptingly over the chair and retreats to the green calm of the living room, watching the flames rising up the chimney and the logs spitting. Rage tears her up inside. How dare she do this; how dare she be so nasty, and in front of Clive? Alice lets a tear fall; then swipes it away, like she's swatting a fly.

"Why did you say Mother could stay before asking me first?" Alice is angry but they're in the kitchen, below

Mother's room – *their* room – and she's up there, resting, so Alice has to speak quietly.

"I thought it would be okay. I was trying to be nice. She took me to one side – she was really apologetic about it."

"She's trying to split us up, don't you see? That's why she asked you instead of both of us. She knew you'd say yes, and that it would upset me."

"You're being paranoid. Why would she want to split us up?"

"It's what she does. She's never liked anyone I've dated. And this is worse – I *married* you." Alice can tell he doesn't believe her. "You don't know her like I do."

"I think you're over-reacting."

"She can't stay here, Clive."

"What do you want me to do? Have you seen the weather?"

"All right, point taken. But, when the snow clears—"

"Where is she going to go? You heard her. She can't move back in for six months."

Alice sighs. The in-law from hell, that's what Alice's ex called her. *I'd marry you,* he'd said, *in a heartbeat. But I couldn't survive your mother.*

"She has to go," Alice says.

"Why is she my problem? She's your mother!"

"We have to *get rid of her.*"

"What are you suggesting?"

Alice feels her stomach knotting. Neither of them answers his question.

As the week comes to an end the snow shows no signs of abating. Great drifts of it pile against the high brick walls of the garden, swept into ice-cream-like swirls by a gathering wind.

Each time they sit at the table, or in the living room, it's the same: Mother picking away at her, criticising her clothes, her cooking, her coffee-making skills, even the way she lights the fire – "No, no, you don't do it *like that*, you're putting too many logs on," insisting on playing that wretched Dean Martin song, even though Christmas has passed and it's New Year's Eve tomorrow night.

She can't stay here for six months. Alice can't cope. She and Clive are arguing and they've never argued before. She can't lose him, she just can't. The idea of life without him is unthinkable. He's *The One*. That's why Alice said yes to him; she just knew – it felt right.

She thinks back to their brief courtship – dating for three months then drunk at a party one night, Clive's rash proposal, her rash acceptance; married two months later. *Soon, too soon*, her friends said. But what do they know?

It's New Year's Eve. Alice is pouring a Baileys, and Clive is sitting on the sofa watching Casualty. Mother appears in the doorway.

Alice looks her up and down, staring at her in disbelief. "How could you?"

"Well, it doesn't fit you, so I thought it would be shame to waste it." Mother folds her toned arms over the green silk.

Alice bites back tears. She is not going to cry. She will not give Mother the satisfaction. She turns away, picks up her drink and sits down next to Clive. *She* enjoys *Casualty* because she likes playing Guess the Accident and Name the Mystery Illness.

"You can't watch this rubbish," Mother says, seating herself on the chair next to her.

"Tell her, Clive. She's being selfish."

Before Alice can stop her, she flicks the channel over, to a gardening programme.

Weeks of this are simmering inside her, like the sprouts on the slow cooker. Alice clenches her fists.

"She was always like this," Mother says. "When she was little, always had to have her own way."

"It's only a television programme," Clive says. "You can watch *Casualty* on Catch Up, can't you?"

Clive is standing in the doorway and in that moment, Alice hates him. She hates the man she can't live without.

"Watch what you want, I don't care." Alice slams out of the room, shaking the door in its frame. She heads upstairs and when she gets to their temporary bedroom, she throws herself onto the bed, pummelling the pillows with her clenched fist and weeping into the feathered down. In that moment she knows what she has to do.

Tomorrow, it's New Year. Alice has at least one resolution she is determined to keep.

New Year's Day is a bright morning, the snow still thick. It has snowed again in the night. Alice goes downstairs to put the kettle on, filling a mug with coffee. There's no sign of Clive.

Anxiety bites again and she fails to push it away. There's no sign of Mother either.

Frowning she pulls up a chair next to the AGA. It's burning on a low heat. It's almost out of coal. Clive usually tops it up when he gets up. She looks out of the French windows. The snow has piled up against them and turned the trees into fat listless figures.

At the side of the garden, a few yards away from the window she's surprised to make out a large snowman, jammed up against the fence. She can just make it out, through the blizzard. Surprised, she wonders how it got there. It's probably Clive, who turns into a big child when it snows.

165

She's thinking about Dan, her childhood sweetheart, her first proper boyfriend. They'd dated throughout school, all through sixth form. She was *so-oo* in love with him – the only person to match that was Clive. But Mother wore Dan down. She carped and sniped, went on at him about his job prospects.

"Do you think you're up to the job of dating my daughter?" she'd say to him, like a matriarch from a Jane Austen novel. "What are your ambitions?" On it went. Until eventually he took her to one side and split with her. Alice was heartbroken but Mother was pleased. "He wasn't good enough for you," she said, not bothering to disguise the victory in her voice.

Alice never really got over him, not until she met Clive. *Where is he?* She's about to get up and check the wardrobe, to see if his clothes are still there when the door goes.

"Clive!" She gets up.

"You really ought to get some fresh air, you're looking quite pasty."

Alice's heart plummets into her slippers.

"Where's Clive?"

Mother gives Alice a strange look. "He's gone, love."

"What do you mean, *gone*? Gone where?"

She's looking out of the window. Alice follows her gaze. The blizzard has subsided and she goes to the window, pressing her face against the cool glass. There it stands, the snowman, with its currant-eyed stare; next to it an over-turned wheel barrow. A hand juts out of the snow, the fingers outstretched; wire binding the wrist to the fence. In the pale winter light, the glint of gold on the finger.

She feels the blood draining from her face.

"It's for the best," Mother says. She wanders off into the kitchen, humming *Winter Wonderland.* The kettle goes on. The snow begins again.

Alice picks up a log from the log basket. She creeps into the kitchen and stands behind Mother, her arms raised.

About the author
Julia has previously published a non-fiction book, *The Resurrection of Oscar Wilde: A Cultural Afterlife* (Lutterworth Press, 2007). Her short stories have appeared in anthologies, including, *Exhausting a Place in Leicester*, (Lulu, September 2019), *Songs for the Elephant Man* (Mantle Lane Press, October 2019), *In the Kitchen*, (Dahlia Press, 2020) and *Dark and Light* (Ruler's Wit, date to be announced). She has had stories shortlisted for *No Spiders were Harmed in the Making of this Anthology, 2020*, and the Hastings Short Story Prize, 2020. She has been a regular contributor for *Journals of a Pandemic*, and *Pendemic*, two online Covid-themed projects.

Time and Tide

Janet Haworth

Gerry swung the steering wheel hard left too late. He crashed into a freshly-painted bollard.

The blue Audi hire car now had a dent in its front fender and an ugly red smear across its paintwork. Sandy resisted expressing what she thought of her husband's driving and ill humour. Gerry had ignored her protests that the other cars were locals and were displaying permits. He had followed the two drivers through an ancient gateway and headed for the Piazza 40 Martiri where he met the bollards designed to hamper his progress.

Sandy just could not help joining in with the laughter of the four Italian young men who were seated at the pavement café enjoying a post-siesta espresso, and the show. Gerry turned to face Sandy, his eyes full of anger; face reddening. He unbuckled his seat belt and swung open the driver's door. Surely, he wasn't going to have it out with the Italian lads? But no, he had firmly planted on his head that ridiculous pink hat he always wore on holidays, and stormed off in the opposite direction, without a word to her.

Sandy slid across to the driver's seat, closed the car door and looked briefly over her shoulder to see the direction Gerry had headed. She just caught sight of his pink hat heading for the nearest gate through the ancient walls that encircled the old town. Before she could follow, she would have to reverse the car off the bollard and head for the permitted car park on the outskirts. Then she planned to go in search of Gerry. Gubbio was small, more like a village. He can't have gone far. Resolving matters with the car hire firm and very probably the police would have to wait.

The oppressive heat of midday had diminished and Sandy took her time walking through the gardens. It was hard to believe that during the Second World War, this sleepy medieval town had been the site of a war crime, having found itself embroiled in struggles between the fascists, and the local partisans. A German soldier had been wounded, and his lieutenant killed. Reprisals were called for and forty of the townsfolk paid the price. Only those visitors who bothered to pause as they strolled through the grove would discover their story. Sandy lingered by the mausoleum without venturing inside where she knew there were pictures of each martyr and a short biography. She turned back towards the gate into the old town. Along the edge of her walk stood the remains of a wall. It seemed idiosyncratic until Sandy moved closer and discovered the traces of bullet holes. It was here that the forty martyrs had met their deaths.

She reached the stone gateway which gave entry into the old town and into another time. Here the streets were narrow, edged with tall four and five-storey buildings dating back to the thirteenth century. They offered shade until they opened into a plaza filled with afternoon sun. Already the old men of Gubbio were gathering at a pavement café. Siesta was coming to an end. This was the time for meeting up with old friends. There were cigarettes to be smoked, card games to be played, and of course afternoon espressos to be drunk.

There was no sign of Gerry but could he have lingered here enjoying a Peroni before. Before what? Going in search of her perhaps. Is that where he was now combing the streets looking for her?

Sandy found the café owner tending his coffee machine. She soon realised that he didn't understand a word she was saying. He handed her a tourist map of the town, smiled and shrugged before turning his back on her, and returning to tending his beloved coffee machine. He clearly had customers waiting for their afternoon caffeine fix.

Sandy stood in the centre of the plaza, hands on hips, gazing around. She spotted a bookshop and a sign that read, *English Books Sold Here.* A young woman was busy putting out a couple of chairs and a table, hoping to catch the evening trade.

"Are you English?" asked Sandy.

The young woman turned and smiled. "Is it that obvious? Yes, I'm from London. I'm Teresa. Can I help you?"

"Have you seen a man in a pink hat in a bad temper? He's my husband and I've lost him."

"It so happens that I have. He seemed quite flustered and told me he had to find you because you are due back in Ancona in three hours' time to board the cruise ship, Pandora. He said that you had a misunderstanding about the traffic restrictions in the town."

"More like a flaming row. Any idea where he went?"

"I suggested he should try the Tourist Information Office. It's not far from here. I see you have a town map. I'll mark the route for you. He only left here about ten minutes ago. You could try phoning him."

"I could if he had his phone with him."

"Ah! So he hasn't?"

"His phone is lying on the backseat of our car along with his wallet and passport."

"Well, the two girls in the Tourist Information Office are very helpful and they speak English."

"How did you end up with a bookshop here of all places?"

"Holiday romance fifteen years ago and the rest is history as they say." She handed Sandy her map. "Come back for a coffee when you find your husband. I don't get to see many people from the UK. Gubbio is off the main tourist trail. Foreigners rarely arrive here in coaches with tour guides. The odd independent traveller will every now again bump into Gubbio or perhaps Gubbio bumps into them?"

"Well Gerry has certainly bumped into Gubbio. Thanks for your help and the invitation to coffee. If we ever find each other we will be back."

Gerry had easily found the Tourist Information Office. The Peroni and his stroll through the shady colonnade of the Logge dei Tiratori calmed him. The tourist office was on the opposite corner. Just as Teresa said he received a warm welcome from the two young women. He thought better of telling his full story. It wouldn't look good. Instead, he asked the two assistants where he could find a mobile phone shop. With full Internet-searching function he would be able to find out everything he needed to know. He was handed a map of the town with his route to the shop clearly marked. He set off and took the first left where he spotted a sign. *Gelateria.* Ice cream shop, just tucked down a side street. He fancied a tub of vanilla which would sustain him on the way to the phone shop. The ice cream parlour when he reached it was hidden in its own inner courtyard. Rainbow-coloured cushions on wicker chairs. Bunting strung from the lavender-coloured wisteria draping the walls of the courtyard. It wouldn't take long to polish off a tub of vanilla in such delightful surroundings. Decision made. One tub of vanilla or maybe mint chocolate. His dilemma was resolved by a pretty girl who offered to give him a scoop of each with chocolate sprinkles. How could he resist?

Sandy arrived at the Tourist Office. No sign of Gerry. Damn it, she must have just missed him. One of the assistants asked her if she needed any help.

Sandy's description of a small, round man wearing a pink hat was received with a smile and a nod of recognition. Signor Gerry had wanted to know where the nearest mobile phone shop could be found. The assistant had explained that there was only one such shop in Gubbio and they had marked the route on his map. Sandy reached into her leather shoulder bag and scrabbled around until she found her map and proffered it to the assistant.

"It will probably take him a quarter of an hour to reach the shop," said the girl. "You will easily catch up with him."

Sandy set off in the direction of the mobile phone shop. She glanced at her map as she stood on the corner of the path just by a sign advertising an ice cream parlour. Yes, she was heading in the right direction and she carried straight on through a maze of cobbled streets that climbed steadily to the Palazzo dei Consoli where, as she had expected, she found the mobile phone shop.

She tried the door and then read the sign: *Chiuso.* It should be open but then she remembered the girls in the Tourist Office had warned her that not all the shops in Gubbio opened at the end of siesta. If the lunch had been good, and the day still hot, some proprietors decided not to re-open.

Anyway, why would Gerry want a mobile phone? He had never managed to memorise her mobile number asserting that there was no need, as he could log it into his phone. The one in his jacket sitting on the back seat of the car, along with his wallet and passport. How would he pay for a new phone? He would only have loose change and a few notes on him. He had insisted on leaving their travellers' cheques tucked safely in the Pandora's safe under the watchful eye of the purser.

She was at least a quarter of an hour behind Gerry. Where would he have gone?

What would he do next? Her frustration with his earlier childish behaviour had ebbed and she was worrying. He had very little money, no phone and no passport. How was she to find him? This was supposed to be a trip to relax, make time for one another. The boys had left home and seemed settled, heralding a new chapter of their lives.

She glanced at her watch just as the giant bell in the tower of the Muncipio tolled four. The Pandora would sail at six – no ifs, no buts. This had been explained to them before they left on this ill-fated journey. *Time and Tide waits for no man*, or woman for that matter. Now that her anger had subsided, Sandy was thinking more clearly. She decided that she would head back to the car and collect Gerry's wallet, phone and passport. Why had she not thought of that before? It was an hour and half's drive to the port. They might just make it if the ship didn't leave on the hour.

The ice cream had cooled Gerry down. That and the rest in the shady courtyard. Should he put his feet up and take a little afternoon snooze? Tempting as that was, he picked up his hat and set off for the phone shop. Confident that once he was in possession of a new phone, he would be able to sort everything out. Sandy was his first priority. Where had she got to and what had she done with the car? So much for a relaxing trip, and a chance to resolve their future.

Arriving at the shop the notice *Chiuso* had not changed and it was then Gerry realised a number of things. First that his wallet with cash and credit cards had been tucked into his jacket along with his passport and phone. The last time he saw them they were resting on the back seat of the hire car. There was still time to get back to the tourist office before they closed and seek their help. He had no idea what form that help would take but he thought they

173

were bound to think of something. The two girls had been so friendly.

Sandy took a short cut through the ancient remains of a Roman amphitheatre and reached the car park. It was a lot fuller and she struggled to remember exactly where she had left the Audi. She scanned the parked vehicles it wouldn't be too hard to find. Afterall, how many blue cars with damaged front fenders and red streaks on their paintwork could there be? Eventually she had to acknowledge that the car had gone and with it Gerry's precious things. Who would steal a damaged car? She flopped down onto one of the benches and looked up just in time to see a low loader carrying the Audi leaving the carpark with a police car following.

Of course, those lovely Italian lads had probably been helping the police with their enquiries and the police having taken possession of the car which had been involved in criminal damage, were probably now in search of Gerry. Gerry was probably even now languishing in a Gubbio police cell. That pink hat would have been a dead giveaway. Well at least she now had a good idea where to find him. She extracted the town map from the bottom of her shoulder bag and soon found the location of the police station. It was close by in the Via Cavour. She could be there before five.

Gerry retraced his steps to reach the Tourist Information Office. The two assistants were busy with a party of Irish nuns. He took a seat on the bench by the door. An elderly nun came and sat down beside him. She gave him one of those smiles that invited confidences and before he knew it, he was pouring out the whole story. The crash, the row, his and Sandy's differences about their futures and at this point he found himself searching for a handkerchief. He was overcome by shame and was now increasingly anxious about

Sandy. Most of all he was exhausted and was struggling to think straight. Since his collision with the traffic bollard events seemed to have conspired against him. One after another his best intentions had turned into disasters. The nun who by now had introduced herself as Sister Hannah Mary, handed Gerry a handkerchief decorated with shamrocks. It looked too delicate for blowing a nose, but he did anyway, and screwed it into a ball before offering it back to the sister, who declined it saying she had plenty more where that one came from, adding that you never knew when some poor soul might be in need of a hanky. Her fellow sisters were keeping the assistants fully occupied when Sister Hannah Mary prodded him in the shoulder and drew his attention to the mountain bike hire shop just across the road. With a twinkle in her eyes, she suggested he hire a bike. Gubbio was a small place and he would be able to cover the ground more quickly on a bike. It would give him a better chance of finding his wife. She and her sisters were setting off on a late afternoon walk around the town following in the steps of St Francis and they would keep a look out for a solitary English woman. Gerry's description of Sandy as a woman in her fifties of slim build, wearing a pale blue blouse over a cream-coloured linen skirt should be easy to spot. To be on the safe side, Sister Hannah Mary pressed a small prayer card into his hand. It depicted St Anthony, the patron saint of lost things. Gerry could hardly refuse and tucked it in his back pocket before setting off for the bike hire shop. He had just enough cash to hire a bike.

Fully confident that no-one forgot how to ride a bike (did they?) he was soon off on his ride around the town, hoping to find his wife. They were running out of time.

Sandy had set out for the police station on the Via Cavour when she had a better idea. She turned around and made her way back to the plaza with the bookshop and Teresa. She thought she would persuade her to accompany her to the police station where she could act as an interpreter. Teresa was more than happy to help. A quick phone call arranged for her mother-in-law to come round and mind the shop. So, it was getting on for five when the pair entered the police station where a smartly-uniformed young officer greeted Teresa as an old friend. After a ten-minute rapid exchange in Italian, they were led off to an interview room by Teresa's friend, Giovanni. A discreet knock on the door heralded the arrival of coffee and a plate of Baba cakes. Teresa was delighted and explained to Sandy that these were a local specialty. Essentially a cream bun drenched with a sticky syrup and soaked in rum. Sandy hadn't eaten since breakfast. She reached for a bun and savoured the taste of the rum liqueur, while Teresa explained Sandy's story to Giovanni.

Sandy reached for a second Baba bun as Teresa said that Giovanni would be coming back with the Italian equivalent of an inspector. Was this a good thing? Teresa said she wasn't sure. She thought Gerry would be charged with criminal damage and leaving the scene of an accident. There was also the small matter of a parking fine as the car had been left in a municipal car park for three hours without displaying a ticket. No doubt the hire car company would have something to say about the damage to the Audi.

There was a tap on the door and a uniformed officer entered. Giovanni respectfully opened the door and introduced Inspettore Rossi who reached for Sandy's hand and took it firmly in both of his before turning to Teresa and greeting her like a long-lost cousin, planting a kiss on each cheek. Inspettore then proffered the plate of Baba buns to Sandy. Sandy, anxious not to give offence, reached for her third bun.

There followed another rapid exchange in Italian between Teresa and the inspettore with occasional interjections from Giovanni. Teresa reached for Sandy's hand and squeezed it tight. She explained that the police were searching for Gerry and expected to apprehend him soon. They thought the pink hat would be *useful*. Clearly, he couldn't go far since their car was lodged securely in the police compound in Perugia some 45 km from Gubbio and it would not be released until these matters were resolved. She told Sandy not to worry and suggested she had another Baba bun.

The rum liqueur had begun to take effect and Sandy felt quite *serene*. Another Baba bun seemed a good idea. Teresa explained that Sandy would have to stay in the room at the police station to wait for Gerry. The police were confident that they would find him quickly. After all, how many men wear pink hats? Teresa would have to relieve her mother-in-law who would be anxious to get home to prepare the family evening meal. Giovanni would be coming back with a female officer, Mariella, who would sit with her while she waited for Gerry. Teresa gave Sandy her business card with her telephone number. Then she was gone and was replaced by the female officer who was to keep her company or was she there to guard her?

Gerry had decided to work his way from the central plaza, in ever widening circles until he had covered the town. At least that was the plan. A plan that Gubbio would deny him. The old town was really a village masquerading as a town that had evolved rather than been planned. It consisted mainly of narrow alleyways edged by tall buildings dating back to the thirteenth century. The alleyways would suddenly open out into intimate squares bursting with afternoon sun. The town tumbled down from the top of a mountain rendering the paths steep at times and bumpy as they were cobbled and, in some parts, stepped. His bike ride would not be as easy and enjoyable as he thought.

It was as he was negotiating one such alleyway that he spotted the party of Irish nuns heading in his direction. He tried braking only to find that his brakes did not work. He wrenched the bike this way and that trying to avoid the nuns who were now heading in different directions trying to evade the inevitable collision. Just before he encountered another of those damn bollards positioned at the end of the alleyway, Gerry spotted the police car crawling to a halt. He fell from the bike which now fell upon him. He was trapped. The nuns were advancing to his aid led by Sister Hannah Mary who was waving his pink hat from which he had parted company. The two policemen, having spotted Gerry replacing the hat on his head, advanced towards him.

The tour guide leading the nuns spoke English. An animated conversation with the two police officers followed and the guide explained to Gerry that he was to be arrested for criminal damage and would have to go with the officers who would take him to the local police station.

Gerry didn't understand.

Things made no sense. None of the nuns had been hurt. Even the damn bollard was unscathed. However, the bike had a buckled and bent front wheel. One of the officers was removing his handcuffs from his belt where they were dangling next to his holster. The guide said he would ensure that the bike was returned to the hire shop and that Gerry had better go with the police. He would be able to get everything sorted out at the police station. Gerry doubted this but having noted that the Italian police were armed, realised he had no choice.

Sandy had just finished off the last Baba bun when there was a knock on the door and in came Giovanni followed by Gerry and Inspettore Rossi. Sandy staggered to her feet and gave Gerry a smile before losing her balance and lurching back into her chair.

"Do you come here often?" slurred Sandy giggling. Then the sight of Gerry in handcuffs soon sobered her mood. She reached for a tissue.

Giovanni had never doubted the calming effect of tea on the English. He took Mariella to one side and told her to take Sandy and get her some tea while the inspector sorted out Gerry.

Mariella told Sandy she need not worry. Inspettore Rossi would explain what would have to happen. Sandy looked at her wristwatch, the one Gerry had given her to celebrate their silver wedding. It was a quarter to six. She asked if she could make a phone call to the cruise ship that they were due to board in Ancona in fifteen minutes' time. When she had finished the call, she felt a bit better. The captain had been very kind and explained that they were not the first couple to miss a sailing and they certainly would not be the last. A local tour operator would arrange for them to stay in a hotel in Gubbio over the weekend and contact them on Monday to book a flight home from Perugia. There would be a fee of course.

The door opened and Gerry came in with the inspector. Sandy was relieved to see that her husband was no longer wearing handcuffs and that Teresa had returned. She broke the news that Gerry would have to appear before the magistrate on Monday morning. There would be a fine for breaking the traffic restriction and a fine for failing to display a parking ticket. Once these matters were resolved and fines paid, they would be free to go. Until then Gerry was being bound over to remain in Gubbio until Monday.

Sandy's phone rang. It was the tour agent giving her details of the accommodation that had been booked for them. Teresa knew the owners of the Grotta dell'Angelo and

179

offered to walk with them to the hotel. It was getting on for seven when they bade farewell to Teresa, promising to meet for coffee on Saturday morning.

Their bedroom had a vaulted ceiling beneath which stood a king-sized, antique bed. A wrought iron affair, with lace drapes. Gerry sat down on the bed. He looked done in. There were scratches on his face and hands from the cycle accident. Sandy stretched out her hand. "Are you okay? Those scratches need cleaning." Gerry followed her into the en-suite bathroom, and what a bathroom. Shining white porcelain except for the twin wash hand basins shaped as shells and in a delicate shade of pink. The tiles depicted scenes from Gubbio interspersed with pictures of birds, trees and flowers.

"I am truly sorry that you are going to miss out on the cruise and our anniversary dinner on the Pandora. It's all my fault. I shouldn't have lost my temper. Can you forgive me, Sandy?"

Sandy was tempted to quote the saying, *"Patience is a virtue rarely found in woman and never in men"* but thought she should curb her tendency to sarcasm.

"I know you wanted the cruise to be a surprise so you didn't ask me how I would like to celebrate and actually I don't like cruising. Remember I even got seasick on that canal boat trip."

Sandy was gazing out of an arched window that looked down into the town. "Look the sun is setting and it is turning the stones in the buildings golden. Teresa said people bump into Gubbio and I think I'm glad we did."

Gerry smiled and joined her at the window; tentatively placing an arm around her waist.

"It's quite a place isn't it. I can see now why they have such strict traffic restrictions. It feels as if we have been taken back hundreds of years. You know when we got parted I felt everything was conspiring against us. I even started to suspect this town was hell bent on foiling us finding each other and it got me thinking."

"Oh dear," said Sandy. "Was that a good thing?"

Gerry turned his face towards her. "Yes, I think so. No, I know so. We've reached one of those important crossroads in life. Before we know it, we'll be retired. The boys have left home and they are doing okay. We got something right and we are still together."

"That sounds like the closing of a door. What comes next?"

"Let's discuss that over dinner. I'm starving and you must be too. Oh, by the way how many of those bun things did you have? Whatever were they feeding you. The interview room reeked of rum."

There was a restaurant a short walk from their hotel. They were intrigued by a stone staircase winding down beneath the road leading to the restaurant housed in one of the many underground natural caves that had once served as storerooms and wine cellars. Two hours later they were walking back to their hotel arm in arm. Over dinner they had dared to dream and share those dreams with each other. Sandy had suspected that Gerry was increasingly frustrated with the changes that had swept into the firm when the senior partner's son had taken over. She was surprised that he had already calculated his pay-off and reckoned there was enough to buy a small garden centre. He just hadn't decided how or when he would tell Sandy. They would have to sell the house that had been their family home for most of their married life. He wasn't sure how Sandy would react. The house was only a mid-terrace in London's old docklands. It had been a struggle when they first bought it but now it was worth a small fortune, enough to set them up in the business venture upon which Gerry had set his heart. Sandy wouldn't have to work in the business unless she wanted to. It turned out that she didn't because she had ideas of her own.

Next morning when they were welcomed by Teresa at the bookshop, they were ready to share their ideas with her. Sandy's plan was to work alongside Gerry. She had always wanted to own her own bookshop. Teresa groaned but then became full of enthusiasm as she explained the highs and lows of running a bookshop with a fellow enthusiast.

Before they left, Sandy asked about the light which shone throughout the night in a small chapel on top of the mountain.

"That's Saint Ubaldo who watches over us. You can't leave Gubbio without visiting his basilica."

"Then we'll make sure we go."

Late afternoon. A trip to the basilica. The perfect ending to their adventure, that had clearly proved to be far more of an adventure than they'd intended... what would the kids think when they told then how thanks to a bollard in Gubbio, they would be changing their lives?

Sandy looked at Gerry as they approached the funicular, which turned out to be a gibbet-like cage. At the top, passengers had to leap out while the cage slowed but did not stop.

"I won't leave you again," Gerry muttered. "Stay close."

"Of course. I've had enough adventure for one trip."

When they reached the top Sandy hesitated too long leaving Gerry with no chance of getting off before the cage continued on its journey back down the mountain. Damn it.

The guard let go of Sandy's arm and she turned just in time to catch a glimpse of a pink hat descending the hillside.

About the author
Janet Haworth lives in North Wales and has picked up her pen again during the lockdowns. She has been published in a hospitality trade magazine. Lockdown provided the opportunity for her to self-publish a collection of her poems, *A Tumble of Poems* and an anthology of spooky short stories, *Curious Coincidences*, both available via Amazon. *Time and Tide* is her first attempt at submitting to a publisher.

Tunnelling from Within

Vanessa Horn

Damned trains! I glance up yet again at the display board. *Maida Vale 2 mins.* That statement would be fine apart from the fact that the letters haven't actually altered since their flickering arrival, a quarter of an hour ago. Unlike the usual flash-in, flash-out tube announcements, most of which coincide with the arrival of actual trains. But here – *now* – no such thing in sight. Not even a rumble. And in response, the commuters throng buzzily up and down the platform, agitating and twitching. Numbers increasing by the minute.

I roll my eyes. Bloody hell; if a train doesn't arrive soon, somebody is going to be either a) compacted into the size of a baked bean tin, or b) propelled messily onto the tracks below. I quickly add a rather less dramatic codicil onto this for my own personal situation: c) I am going to be late for work. *Extremely* late. However, I'm not really bothered by that.

I study the billboards lined up along the tunnel: methodically arranged washing on a line. Adverts for plays, musicals, breast enhancing… teeth whitening… a poem… A *poem*. Hmm. I used to enjoy poetry, back when I had time to read. As a teenager, that is, before I was forced to enter my highly-paid, highly-wearisome IT career. Well. I correct myself; to be fair, I wasn't actually *forced* – merely coerced. By my father. He of the reckoning that steady job (long hours with good pay) equals responsible person. He also of the opinion that poetry – both the reading and writing of – was far too frivolous an option. So, having spent my childhood unwilling to disappoint my only parent, on leaving school, I took the route recommended by him. Naturally.

But… this is now. My father is long gone, even though his words still linger. Poetry is here for the taking. The reading. I focus on the overly-large-font text, preparing to savour the words, hoping they will somehow transport me to a different place – a *better* place.

The Fog

I saw the fog grow thick,
Which soon made blind my ken;
It made tall men of boys,
And giants of tall men.

I pause in my reading for a moment, *just* a moment, exhaling deeply. Loudly. In response, the umbrella-carrying man beside me tuts and shuffles backwards slightly. Aha – bonus space! Using the opportunity to move my stiffly-cramping left leg a couple of centimetres, I then gladly return to the poem – the *ethereal* – fog and its sight-robbing, cotton-wool-wrapping features. Is it fate that I find myself so easily identifying with the sentiment here? Or just chance? Huh – probably the latter, I guess. But still…

When I think about fog – the physical fleeciness of it, the way it clams around a person, leaving them uneasy and intimidated, I acknowledge it's the feeling I experience every day – twice a day – surrounded by bodies in this tightly-packed tin can of a station. Oppressed. Restricted. And yes, the commuters around me *are* tall men and giants, enlarged out of proportion by their proximity. Far too many people knitted together in this murky miasma.

However, more frightening, is the fact that this fog – *my* fog – doesn't dissipate, even outside of the tube station. No, my own personal fog follows me from home to work, through the day, back home again and in the evening to come. All-pervading. Omnipresent. I sigh. There's nothing new in being dissatisfied with your life; you could most likely distinguish the same feeling emanating from every person down here. So. No point in dwelling on it. I can't do anything about it. Ignoring the tiny voice inside me, which is unhelpfully saying, "Why not?" I peer hopefully down the tunnel instead. Still no train. I sigh and continue reading.

It clutched my throat, I coughed;
Nothing was in my head
Except two heavy eyes
Like balls of burning lead.

Heavy... Balls of burning lead? I looked away and consider this, simultaneously testing the weight and heat of my eyeballs by rolling them gently side to side. No. I'm not experiencing this, although I can identify with the imagery that the words suggest. Intense. Dramatic. But it's a likeness which would probably better be appropriate to describing my return journeys, riding on the hangover days of screen-staring and number-champing.

But, focusing back on the poem I suddenly realise that the words of the next verse are... *moving?* Yes, moving! Shivering in their previously stoic Times New Roman, they twitch and tremble, like frustrated jellies waiting to be unmoulded. I blink rapidly – *what the?* I quickly look around to assess the reactions of my fellow congestions. Nothing. *They* remain irate and exasperated, shifting and muttering. Focusing on their discomfort. Not, by any means, intrigued. Not like me. They can't see what's going on. Well, then surely it can't be happening; it must be one of those figments that you hear about. An escalation into chaos of an already cluttered and stressed mind. Damn – that's all I need!

185

Slowly – reluctant to prove my theory – I turn my gaze back again to the billboard. Ah – now not only are the words still moving, they're now *dancing!* The whole poem! Like skinny black butterflies, the cursive letters pirouette and plie across and around the large billboard. Woah! Spiralling, twirling, prancing, they seem the very epitome of liberty and nonconformity, here in this tiresome tube station. And yet, fascinated though I am, I can see that there is still a system to their madness; I can still make sense of the verse – the words are travelling in tandem, faithfully following their bidden order:

> *And when it grew so black*
> *That I could know no place,*
> *I lost all judgment then,*
> *Of distance and of space.*

Surreal. And the words themselves... *Lost all judgment.* I think about this. Yes. Ironic, given the nature of what I'm seeing in front of me. Bizarre. Most surprisingly, it's hard to believe that no-one else around me can perceive what's going on... But wait – as I continue to stare at the nomadic words, I'm aware that around me, everything is still. Static. There are no more mutterings, shiftings, the occasional shriek of a child. Not now. Just silence. Tranquillity. What's happening? *How* did it happen?

I turn to the people closest to me – the middle-aged man, a headphone-clad teenager, a young mother clutching her toddler's hand – and realise that each of them is still. Mute, too. Not that that's necessarily a negative, after all the commotion of earlier. Nevertheless... Some strange phenomenon has taken place while I've been so intently watching the dancing words. What has happened? And... why am *I* the only one not rendered immobile, like the rest of them?

186

I inch carefully out of my cramped position and move warily amongst my fellow commuters, taking care not to touch anyone; I'm not exactly sure why. Unless it's that I feel it might break this whole… *spell* that the poem appears to have generated? I can't jeopardise this; it's too uncanny a situation to risk relinquishing just yet.

I peer at the umbrella-toting man who had been standing next to me, moving closer until my face is almost in contact with his. My breath on his cheek. Frozen in the moment, his expression shows the delineations and contours of his existence. Discontent? Worry? Dissatisfaction? Yet his eyes seem to belong to someone younger. Someone who still has hope. Though I perceive – I don't know exactly how – that this hope is decreasing. He's waiting, just waiting. For some*thing*? Some*one*? Only he knows. I wonder whether he'll get his wish, or whether the cruelty of life will take him away just as his fingertips stretch out to touch it. Will his realisation be too late?

Another thought occurs to me: will I be this man, albeit in a decade or so? Will I too have lines of unhappiness and disgruntlement mapped across my face, yet still be doing the things that are causing my misery? God, I hope not. It's a scary concept. One which would certainly bring me to the very brink of despair.

But then it comes to me jerkily, clumsily. Just as the letters in the poem didn't have to remain still, I don't *have* to be this man. I don't have to be experiencing a lifestyle rut. Don't have to be restrained by my own fear. No, *My* realisation can be here, it can be now. Yet… can it? *Dare* I break away, when I can still hear my late father's counsel in my inner mind? But, conversely, if I *don't* try, will the moment ever return? Is this my only window of opportunity? Will I instead end up bitter and fearful, stuck in a tedious job – *life*, even – blaming others for my lack of decisiveness?

187

No. My mind is finally made up – I'm going to do this. It will happen; I'll make it materialise. And, now that they've been given permission, mischievous thoughts flutter about my mind, suggesting and urging, skipping and surging. The way I can do this... I have savings now, from my years of toil. I can leave my job, leave my rented flat. Maybe I'll travel down to Cornwall, start a new life there. Yes, by the sea where the muttering waves and gull-pocked sky will inspire me, and allow the words to dance once more inside my head. It's a risk but it's one I'm now ready to take. After all, if I don't then I'll never know if it could be done. It's time.

Just about to leave, though, I suddenly have a thought: surely I shouldn't just go without trying to help anyone else here in the tube station? I need to help the others, if possible. I scrabble inside my jacket pocket, eventually locating a board marker: thick black. Quickly uncapping the lid, I bend down and scrawl a message in large letters on the concrete platform:

READ THE POEM

Done. It might work; who knows? Nonetheless, at least I've tried. I smile. Relief? Yes, indisputably. I've made my decision; I'm off, off far away to watch the ocean – away to read poetry. To write poetry. I resolve to leave all my obligations – my *burdens* – alongside the tube tracks, right here. I've done my time; now it's my turn.

As I leave the station, I glance back over my shoulder, observing that the commuters have shuddered back into motion, resuming their muttering and complaining, seemingly unaware that they were – temporarily – frozen in time. And the poem? Yes, that's back in its rightful place too, static and reconciling. I wonder, absently, if the last few verses contain any further messages of advice. But... I

188

don't *need* to know. I've got what I desired. The poem's work is done.

About the author

Vanessa Horn is a Junior School teacher who first became interested in writing in 2013, when she took a sabbatical year off from work. Since then, she has written several hundred stories, many of which have been published in magazines, and others having won prizes in short story and flash fiction competitions. In 2015, her first book *Eclectic Moments* – a collection of short stories – was published by Alfie Dog Fiction.
www.bookdepository.com/Eclectic-Moments-Vanessa-J-Horn/9781909894273

Since venturing into writing for children two years ago, Vanessa's picture book – *Waaaaaa,* published by Tiny Tree Books – was released in January 2020.
www.matthewjamespublishing.com/products/tiny-tree/waaaaaa

In May 2020, Vanessa's collection of flash fiction for adults – *Theme and Variations* – was published by Chapeltown Books. https://smarturl.it/6s1tqp. This is a compilation of stories all based on or around the theme of music.

Unseen Eyes

Linda Flynn

*The resolution to avoid an evil is seldom framed till
the evil is so far advanced as to make avoidance
impossible.*

Thomas Hardy

You always know when you are being watched. There's
that sense of a tingling in your spine, a boring into your
back, or an awareness that every detail is being observed.
And all without you turning around.

Most of the time you would brush it away, forgotten,
like the litter blowing across the platform. At other times
you might freeze, knowing that you are almost alone, as you
try to focus on the peeling posters. The train rushes in like
an indrawn breath and you leap on.

You know it's not unusual, it happens to everyone, so
why is it troubling you today?

A quick glance around the carriage, without making
any eye contact, assures you that everything is normal:
faces buried in newspapers, books or phones, a pale
pensive man twisting some interview notes in his lap, a
ginger-haired girl impatiently kicking her legs against the
seat, figures stood at the poles turned away from each
other. Then the deep, dark blur of the tunnel as the
windows gleamed back dull reflections. So why is your
heart beating a little faster?

You rub your eyes; you hadn't slept well last night,
haunted by the shadowy outline by the bush outside your
bedroom window.

The train seems to wait ages at the station. It's hard not
to drum your fingers as passengers heave on and off. An

obstruction in the doors. At last it surges forward and those standing sway backwards.

You scan the new faces, clenching your hands which are now clammy with dread.

You see a black jacket weaving through the passengers. It's the same as a thousand other black jackets seen on the underground, but there's something in the straightness of the back, an alertness, and the air around you feels suffocating.

Of course neighbours meet each other all the time: chance encounters buying a pint of milk, collecting a newspaper, walking a dog. But still, not all the time, not the exact same routine.

You should have taken a taxi. Too late to think of that now.

The hooded mac helps. Not your usual raincoat. You don't even like it much, but bland beige blends in.

The train screeches to the penultimate stop before you must disembark. Your heart is hammering. You glance down at your shoes. Not ideal for walking.

You hold your breath and in your head begin counting the three seconds it will take for the doors to fully close. Then you leap out at one, forcibly parting people as you sprint on to the platform.

A hurried glance behind; then breathe. You flit into the gap between commuters, knowing the space will close as people jostle forward.

Before you reach the escalator you slip off your coat, scrunch it into a ball and shove into your bag. Black clothes. Good.

Your heart is thumping but you must take the escalator calmly, without drawing attention to yourself; so you ease in front of a bulky man and remain motionless, steadying your pulse.

The crowd on the pavement outside has thinned, so you slip inside a busy shop, slide past customers and out of a side door. It's all time lost and you will be late for work; if only you had left slightly earlier today.

There's the reassuring rumble of traffic and once more you are swallowed up by a group of pedestrians. You keep pace with them – there's safety in numbers. Everyday conversations flitter around you, dull and reassuring, people going about their everyday lives.

You try to resist turning your head around, checking, watching. With an effort of will you face mainly forwards, throwing the occasional glance at reflections in shop windows. There's nothing unusual and you are nearly there.

As you approach the main door to your office your knees feel weak with relief and you long to sit down.

Instinct makes you twist your head slightly towards the café window opposite. Then you see him. He gives a half smile and seems to raise his coffee cup in greeting.

He was there before you. He already knew where you worked.

You thought you had noticed when you were being watched, but you hadn't, not really. Another detail had been given away, another piece of the jigsaw puzzle that formed your life, another fact gleaned from following, making you easier to stalk.

About the author
Linda Flynn has had books published for children and teenagers as well as twenty-one short stories, mainly written for adults. She can be found at www.lindaflynn.com.

Waiting Out the Winter

Amy B Moreno

I pull the duvet further up over my knees, exposing the end of the bed; sheet the colour of faded flesh stretched over it. I pinch at a bobbled patch on my left, piling the balls into a tufty wee pyramid. The miniatures in the fridge giggle and chatter together. Except they don't, because nobody laughs in this waiting place.

The rattle and clatter of a trolley approaches down the hall, nearing my door. The hall which may as well be a long-haul flight + connecting flight + domestic flight away and back again. I can't go out there. My fingers splay on top of the pyramid, imitating the many-legged insect in the hall, fumbling to control the wheels with its skittery limbs. If I pushed a trolley, it would be piled high with fluffy, snowy towels, warm from the industrial dryers. I hear them, rumbling through the night; an ever-hungry tummy in the basement.

I breathe in this stuffy air, as I lie – stuffed with scentless room service bread rolls. The crumbs tattletale that I overate in bed again; another crime to repent. I will leave my tray outside the door at 10 am precisely. I will push at the navy-blue hall carpet with my bare foot. I will hunch my shoulders and look from side to side, like a crow with its knees on backwards, to check for the hotel staff; knowing I will not see anyone.

What I do keep seeing are flies, just outside my field of vision. I feel the flick of their wings on my bare skin. I swat at one with the back of my hand, then wipe it along the sheet.

The red light on the telly winks. My phone beeps. The weak February sun tap-taps at the pane. My three windows from the outside reach out and pull at the hem of my nightie for attention (and no, of course I'm not dressed yet). Really, I am too hot, but I wrap the duvet over my shoulders and around my body, enjoying the image; a little fat caterpillar, eating her way through a week and a half. I shuffle to the window, playing this part of an invalid. I step so close to the glass that my nose is pressed flat. The rest of my face follows, squashing out a grimace that my youngest would love. I step to the left, away from the guilt, and watch below.

So far below this ladder of boxed-in rooms: the criss-cross people, and the stop-start buses, sledging through snow trails. I run my hand around the edge of the frame – no cold draught. I do not breathe their icy air. In this room, I breathe my own hours over and over. In these ten days of blank pages, and brittle bird feet in the snow, and broken mistakes, I am removed, and I wait the decision.

I spent four days outside of the wall calendar scribbles, where I slipped into short-sleeves, and those sun-warmed arms. Four days when I left my phone in the drawer of the bedside cabinet; where I didn't sterilise dummies; or wring out snow-sodden jackets; or bare a train track of milk teeth bite marks along my arm. Four days when I picked up not one thing that another person had thrown on the floor. Four days of gentle sun in my empty hands. Four days which I told Tom about in a scribbled kitchen table note.

Then they informed me there would be ten more days, upon my arrival. Ten days of watching and waiting and not knowing what Tom will say or what he has told the boys. Ten days of clasped hands and penance. But what would I have done without those four days away from the long winter and all its demands?

The winter was never my kind of season. I always considered it the most narcissistic – it serves only itself. The

194

winter is more needy than it thinks – it would never survive on its own. And it displays itself like an open book – "Oh, look at me, I know myself so well, I have nothing to hide, I lay everything bare." Well, I don't want to see your rickly tree trunk ribs or your po-faced puddles. There are things that should remain hidden, kept for yourself; not handed out like fairground tokens. Things that remind me of myself that I stuff deep in my pockets, where little hands try to reach in a grab at them.

Far better the independence of summer. Fully covered, she can pretend to be something else, if it takes her fancy (and it should). She can wear this wild rose or that honeysuckle, swept around into a feather boa. She can dress her life as someone else's – even if it's just for a long weekend.

Besides that, winter presents a trio of toothless sludgy meals in bowls – porridge, soup, stew. And perpetually damp coat sleeves. That nails on blackboard scrape and swear of credit card on frosted windshield. And always taking my gloves off to wipe snottery noses, and fix buggy clips, and pick up special sticks and all the other things that I've dropped around me.

All the things I've dropped around me.

No, not for me, the winter.

On my final night in this waiting room, the snow melts. The ants run all over my body. And I scratch out all the badness. I throw the duvet from the bed, and let my arms and legs and wings stretch to all four corners of the room. I am awake no earlier than usual, which sets me on edge as today should be different to the others, should it not? I try to find my excitement in the suitcase, repacked with the same sets of nightclothes I have rotated these past two weeks. I've binned the remaining complementary shampoo bottles – they feel sticky and contaminated. I don't want to touch anything else in this room now. I leave my shrivelled cocoon on the bathroom floor, twisted up in the bathmat.

At 9am, there is a muffled dunt at the door, as if the person has used their elbow instead of their knuckles. I turn the handle, and a masked and badged official, wafts up from the hall carpet – a continuation in navy blue. It stands two metres back, pressed against the wall. It's positioned between two faded water colours; an interrupting portrait.

I pull my bag and the wheels squeak back. The hall feels longer than I remembered and holds that smell of Thursday afternoon in a staffroom – old coffee, tired feet, nervous desperation. I follow around, down, then into a lobby, so high-ceilinged.

Sensible, flat-soled feet push a rattling trolley back where I came from.

Navy Suit hands me some release paperwork and I am alone.

Is that it? Is it over? I push through the exit door and it closes unsatisfyingly slowly and gently behind me. A wind slaps me in the face – that's better. Its brother runs up my nose and pokes at the back of my eyes. It pushes out the must, the yeasty rolls, flushes out the bottled rose, out of season. It smells of nothing but cold. Icy threads make their way up the sleeves of my too-thin linen jacket. I find a frozen puddle and my sandal slides left then right, wiping everything clean. I can start again.

Tom beeps at me with harassed eyebrows. The inside of the car looks like one of those grab-a-toy claw games at the shows. A clutter of car seats and sticky faces peek out from under the mess. One of them starts greetin'. Tom doesn't leave the car. I roll over and open the door.

"I'm so sorry," I say.

Some Scots words:

rickly – rickety; ramshackle; tottering
snottery – covered with snot
to dunt – to gently bump
greetin – crying

About the author

Amy B. Moreno writes poetry and fiction for adults and children, in English, Scots, and Spanish, including multilingual pieces. She has recently been published in *Mslexia*, *The London Reader*, *The Common Breath*, and *Glittery Literary* (children's anthology). New picture book, *A Billion Balloons of Questions*, coming in spring 2022.

Twitter: @Amy_B_Moreno

Like to Read More Work Like This?

Then sign up to our mailing list and download our free collection of short stories, *Magnetism*. Sign up now to receive this free e-book and also to find out about all of our new publications and offers.

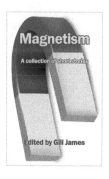

Sign up here:
  http://eepurl.com/gbpdVz

Please Leave a Review

Reviews are so important to writers. Please take the time to review this book. A couple of lines is fine.

Reviews help the book to become more visible to buyers. Retailers will promote books with multiple reviews.

This in turn helps us to sell more books... And then we can afford to publish more books like this one.

Leaving a review is very easy.
Go to https://smarturl.it/2qu4f4, scroll down the left-hand side of the Amazon page and click on the "Write a customer review" button.

Other Publications by Bridge House

Mulling It Over

edited by Debz Hobbs-Wyatt and Gill James

The Island of Mull, covered in mulls. To mull a drink. An important instrument for making a book. Plenty to mull over here. And plenty to make you think.

As ever, the interpretation has been varied: the Island of Mull, thinking about things, often quite deeply, the odd mulled drink and even something used in making a book - how appropriate again. You will find a variety of styles here and an intriguing mix of voices. There is humour and pathos, some hard-hitting tales and some feel-good accounts. All to be mulled over.

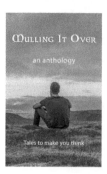

"The Island of Mull is a great concept - we all have had plenty to mull over in 2020. It's a great collection of stories. Very well done!" (*Amazon*)

Order from Amazon:

Paperback: ISBN 978-1-907335-93-8
eBook: ISBN 978-1-907335-94-5

Nativity

edited by Debz Hobbs-Wyatt and Gill James

Many of the stories in this collection take place at or near
Christmas time. There are stories of new births, of rebirths,
of new beginnings, and there are a couple that deal with the
joys and sorrows of the annual Nativity Play.

There are some familiar authors in this volume and also some
new writers. We treasure them all.

"A most unexpected collection of stories, focused on new
beginnings and rebirth. It's definitely not your traditional
nativity theme, but so much more. The stories are so varied,
dramatic, melancholic, dark and comedic, there is a story to
suit everyone." (*Amazon*)

Order from Amazon:

Paperback: ISBN 978-1-907335-76-1
eBook: ISBN 978-1-907335-77-8

Crackers

edited by Debz Hobbs-Wyatt and Gill James

Every year we pick a very vaguely Christmas-related theme for our annual anthology. Then we invite our writers to subvert it. In this collection, they've certainly done that to the extent that we almost had a picture of cream crackers for the cover. Our theme this year is "crackers". So, we have Christmas crackers, cream crackers, cracking dresses, a cracked antique and many, many other interpretations. We hope you will find this a cracking good read.

"A wonderfully quirky and eccentric collection of short stories. Each one has a different take on the notion of 'crackers' with a heart of darkness resonating throughout. A book of little morality gems!" (*Amazon*)

Order from www.bridgehousepublishing.co.uk

Paperback: ISBN 978-1-907335-59-4
eBook: ISBN 978-1-907335-60-0

Lightning Source UK Ltd.
Milton Keynes UK
UKHW020658070922
408471UK00010B/1081